Vincent Crow: Export

Vincent Crow: Export

D.C.J. Wardle

Copyright © 2014 D.C.J. Wardle

The moral right of the author has been asserted.

Apart from any fair dealing for the purposes of research or private study, or criticism or review, as permitted under the Copyright, Designs and Patents Act 1988, this publication may only be reproduced, stored or transmitted, in any form or by any means, with the prior permission in writing of the publishers, or in the case of reprographic reproduction in accordance with the terms of licences issued by the Copyright Licensing Agency. Enquiries concerning reproduction outside those terms should be sent to the publishers.

Matador
9 Priory Business Park,
Wistow Road, Kibworth Beauchamp,
Leicestershire. LE8 0RX
Tel: (+44) 116 279 2299
Fax: (+44) 116 279 2277
Email: books@troubador.co.uk
Web: www.troubador.co.uk/matador

ISBN 978-1783063-215

British Library Cataloguing in Publication Data.
A catalogue record for this book is available from the British Library.

Typeset by Troubador Publishing Ltd, Leicester, UK

Matador is an imprint of Troubador Publishing Ltd

Printed and bound in the UK by TJ International, Padstow, Cornwall

For Jill.

Thanks to Cathy for all the support.

Chapter 1 – Travel

Flight

The overhead seatbelt signs went off. This was accompanied by a 'ping' from somewhere nearby in the aircraft. It was as if elevator music had been compressed down into a single annoying sound, ready to become the light entertainment version of the big bang and spew out an eternal cosmos of soprano saxophones.

Despite the sudden change in cabin status, the no-smoking signs above them remained firmly illuminated. To Vince's knowledge it had been several years since anyone had been allowed to smoke on an international or domestic flight, so he couldn't understand why the unchangeable option was displayed at all. It struck Vince that this was very unfair to the smokers on the plane. Having this very specific information about their addiction illuminated directly above every seat created the false hope that at some stage they might eventually become un-illuminated, so everyone could rush to the back of the plane and light up. Not only did it serve smokers as a constant reminder that they were craving the opportunity to smoke, but it was one of hundreds of airline rules about things that you couldn't do – so why single this one out?

The 'ping' singularity not only changed the seatbelt status for the on-board passengers but, for a middle-to-aging gentleman a few rows up from Vince, it acted like the trigger word from a prior hypnotism. He sprung up from his seat and immediately started rummaging intensely for something vital in the overhead luggage compartment. His determination to avoid the effort of actually taking the bag down and looking inside it meant that soon he was on tiptoe and his whole arm and shoulder had disappeared inside, drawn into the overhead locker as if he was in a dodgy ventriloquist act pretending that his mischievous puppet was dragging him in. Vince noticed that further up the plane on the other aisle a comparably aged gentleman was performing a similar and urgent comedy routine.

It must be just something you have to do on planes at that stage in life, Vince decided.

To Vince's right, Natalie was already half asleep, her neck bent at an uncomfortably awkward angle and dribbling slightly on to the glossy duty-free magazine. Her saliva was staking a claim on a bottle of perfume that she was planning to put on her credit card once the air stewardesses started selling. To Vince's left was his nan, staring through her thick-lensed glasses with extreme intensity and agitation at the no-smoking sign that continued to blaze above her.

"Must be something wrong with it, Vince. Wiring probably. Last thing you need on something as technom-logically technical as an aeroplane is dodgy wiring. Mrs. Barry had some electrician in last year re-doing her wiring 'cos the man from the council said it was pre-war and it had to be pulled out. A month later her pissin' TV overheated, and she had to call him out again."

"I'm just getting up to go to the loo, Nan. They'll probably bring food soon."

"On a Sunday it was, and he wouldn't come round to have a look 'til the next day. She had to go all round the pissin' house unplugging everything, and then just sat there in the pissin' dark all night."

"I'll be back in a minute, Nan."

Vince climbed carefully over the snoring Natalie, gently mopping her chin with his complementary wet-wipe after he did so.

It was going to be another twelve hours until their transit stop. Vince had heard from one of the bar-proppers in the Carrot and Jam Kettle that if you travel from London to Asia by plane then you actually loose five or six hours on account of the earth still spinning while you were up there. If that meant less time learning about Mrs. Barry sitting in the pitch black to avoid TV-induced electrocution then shortening his life by six hours was a reasonable price to pay.

Abroad

Vince had only ever been to Wales when it came to being 'abroad'.

When you're about ten, and you're comparing far flung foreign adventures into the unknown with other compatriots of a similar level of life experience, then Wales definitely counts in the 'abroad' stakes. No doubt about it. When you've reached your twenties, however, and are suffering some backpacker's tedious monologue of their egotistically mind-broadening 'year out', which included six-months discovering themselves spiritually in remote corners of Peru by banging on a drum with some other stoned teenagers, then bringing up Wales isn't going count as proof of an equal footing. Even if you do have photographic evidence that demonstrates you were there for a whole week at the beach, and it didn't rain once, the first time that had happened 'in, like, ever' (or at least since pre-Cambrian times).

As Vince stepped off the plane at Feiquon's international airport, he decided that Wales really was a very different kind of abroad to the one he was in now. In retrospect, he now realised that the conversation he'd once had with an arrogant young returnee from Peru at the bar in the Carrot and Jam Kettle, where he defended the notion that a weekend camping in the Mumbles was a comparable adventure to a trek through the Peruvian rainforests, was based on a marginally floored hypothesis.

The wall of Feiquon heat and humidity that engulfed him on the steps of the plane was a shock to the system. He was mopping the sweat from his brow before he'd even descended to the tarmac. The uncomfortable stickiness was almost worse than working in the kitchens at the Carrot and Jam Kettle on a busy Friday night in the summer, stench of chip-fat aside.

Behind him Natalie was liberally applying her new duty-free perfume, and behind her his nan was standing in the oval doorway of the plane with a lighter in one hand and a cigarette in the other. The limited pace at which her aging frame could propel her forward in a straight line meant that the distance from the aeroplane steps to the door of the immigration lounge was definitely at least one fag's-worth.

Back in the UK, the excitement for Vince of getting a passport for the first time had also meant that he'd sent all their passports to the Feiquon Embassy in London to get their business visas approved. Therefore, traversing immigration and baggage claim was relatively straight forward compared to the other tourists and backpackers.

Vince negotiated his way through the airport, past the authorities and into the untamed wilderness beyond. As he did so he found that his lack of indigenous language skills was the next obstacle to reinforce his new appreciation of the different levels on the scale of 'being abroad'.

Vince had tried to bluff a degree of control in his position of group leader as they made their way through arrivals, feeling that the constant repetition of the word 'taxi' would address their upcoming need for additional transport. Despite this effort, a moped drawn cart which he understood to be a 'tuk-tuk' was the unlikely form of transport with which he was presented. As Natalie, Vince, Vince's nan, and their considerable luggage were all squeezed into the mini-sized carriage, it seemed even less roomy than it had on first inspection. The very fact that they had agreed to this form of transport rather than a more conventional taxi was fairly perplexing to Vince. There had been an official-looking person in the arrival area whose primary role in society had seemed to be supporting people to find rides into town. The man had clearly achieved a sufficient grasp of what Vince had been saying to understand the name of the guesthouse in Khoyleng they were booked into, as well as what price he was going to charge them for a go in his chariot. So, with that level of understood communication, how had they then ended up in this thing? Until now, Vince had believed 'taxi' to be one of the few words that transcended all languages and cultures: like 'dollar' or 'okay', or 'Beckham'.

"Your grand-dad used to have a three-wheeler. Motorcycle with a sidecar, Vince. Green one."

Vince looked towards the pile of luggage on the opposite seat to locate the source of the muffled observation. It was reassuring to hear that his nan was still apparently with them, even if he couldn't actually see her.

"Not like this pissin' cart-drawn nonsense though! Mind

you, he had it in pieces in the kitchen most of the time, getting oil everywhere. That new kitchen of Mrs. Reynolds' has only been done eighteen months and the doors are already coming loose on the pissin' cupboards. Probably that pissin' foreign rubbish they get from Scan-dum-navium."

Vince was starting to wonder how his nan would cope in a place like Feiquon. A wobbly cupboard door in Mrs. Reynolds' kitchen, with a design that may or may not have links to another neighbouring country within Europe was her main preoccupation, having arrived in an exotic new land. On this basis, how was she going to cope with being in a foreign country, where almost everything was probably far more foreign than Mrs. Reynolds' new cupboards.

Fortunately, Natalie waded in to rescue Vince from pondering over this dilemma any further:

"That's all that bloomin' cheap pinewood rubbish they import, Nan. We're in the tropics now. That's where all the proper big wood grows in the first place. They'll have proper heavy cupboard doors in all the kitchens out here."

Whereas Vince, over the years, had got used to considering his nan's contributions to shared discourse as entirely rhetorical, Natalie had recently got into the habit of actually responding to his grandmother's non-sequiturs, as if they were parts of genuine conversations.

Vince smiled approvingly at his astute girlfriend. Her ill-informed but highly confident geographical insight regarding equatorial flora had overpowered his nan's random drivel in the same way that the rather pungent perfume that Natalie had bought on the flight was overpowering the scent of their combined sudden need to perspire excessively in the tropical heat. Between the three of them, they would be quite a team as they took on the exciting business world of Asia. Well, apart from his nan of course.

The plan

Vince's financial sponsor in the new foreign business venture was a Mr Jonathan Fairchild: a rich American businessman with a penchant for benevolence and Mexican revolutionaries, peppered with a degree of gullibility, and a generously proportioned moustache.

Vince and Fairchild had first become acquainted the previous year whilst they were both in London. At the time, Vince had been rigidly following his self-imposed self-improvement plan of 'trading-up'. It was an ingenious scheme that meant he had to trade up his life every three months for a new and better one. Not just moving up the ladder to a better job, he had to trade-up everything for a completely different life, and that included the pad, the girlfriend, the clothes, and the car.

Since their first meeting, Jonathan Fairchild had been embroiled in a number of Vince's schemes, both directly and indirectly. However, the current plan that had brought Vince and his family to Asia had resulted very much from one of Fairchild's whims, rather than anything that Vince had cooked up.

The previous year, Fairchild had travelled to Asia with his new found love, Susan, and they had married on some far-flung exotic and sandy beach before returning to his yacht for post matrimonial cocktails and vol-au-vents. Asia had therefore embedded itself in the mind of Jonathan Fairchild as a location for success and achievement. Characteristically, Fairchild's enthusiastic tendency for entrepreneurism tended to mirror the geography of perceived and recent success. The erratic association between achievement and the location where it all happened meant that his previously ill-conceived London-based fad of becoming an English Gent had waned dramatically, and his interest in exotic Asian enterprises had waxed considerably. It was arguably for this reason that Vince now found himself in the heat of Feiquon with a view to starting up a chain of guesthouses for his long-standing American benefactor.

The business plan for Jonathan Fairchild, as an investor, was simple enough. He would dabble in the Asian hospitality trade and the dabbling would, in turn, generate entertaining stories for him to ramble about at boring social events. Meanwhile, Vince would head out to Asia and as Fairchild's man in the field, find a mid-range guesthouse and take over the lease for a few months. This would be a trial run. Vince and Natalie would use this experience to study the intricacies of Feiquon guesthouse management from both a legal and practical perspective. They needed to understand licensing laws, leasing bylaws, employment laws and so forth. From a practical side, they needed to understand the tourism sector to identify where the market gaps were, and the demands in terms of services, cuisine and location. They also needed to get to grips with more immediate practical understandings with regard to water, waste disposal, power and finally the recruiting of an efficient and professional staff for them to work with. In theory, it all seemed straight-forward enough.

Vince was pleased to be working for Fairchild. At the same time, putting at least a continent's distance between Vince and Fairchild's immediate entourage, whilst pursuing this daring business venture had its distinct advantages. This was not due to Fairchild, for whom Vince carried a high degree of respect and gratitude. It was more that Fairchild's new bride was something of a ferocious dragon. Even Saint George would have steered clear if he'd been presented with the choice of slaying this aggressive and fearsome mythical beast as an optional module whilst trying to accumulate sufficient credits to be awarded his sainthood. Vince had crossed paths with Susan on a number of occasions. The more remote the likelihood of any additional path crossing, the more secure Vince felt.

Getting started

Vince had arrived in Feiquon's capital city, Khoyleng – so that was where he would begin. His local knowledge of Khoyleng was as vacant and clean a slate as anywhere else in the country, but it did have the advantage of being the place where fate had enabled him to turn up first of all. There was no benefit in leaving the unknown for another unknown without being able to judge the relative advantage of either. Having eventually checked in to the hotel the previous night, the weary and sweaty travellers were able to wholeheartedly embrace the benefits of the power-hungry air-conditioning. Any shallow sentiments they may have harboured towards the fragility of the environment, cute fluffy mammals, or devastating ocean pollution were immediately abandoned in favour of this fuel-guzzling life-saver.

Natalie's previously upbeat enthusiasm for their exotic business venture had slipped a little since they had disembarked onto foreign soil. Vince had identified the uncomfortable and sweaty tuk-tuk ride as the catalyst for this change in attitude. The increasing complaints from Natalie, including her disapproval of the heat, the humidity, the flies, the insects, the traffic and the pollution had led Vince towards the realisation that she was a little out of her comfort zone, and probably needed some time to adjust.

Unfortunately, Natalie's comfort zone was one where 'outside' was a necessary evil to be treated with considerable caution, if not contempt. It was only to be ventured in if it was essential to get from the pub to a shoe shop and then back again. Shopping malls were therefore a god-send for Natalie, as she could normally get into the car in her own garage, drive to a multi-storey car-park and then access the shops, all without being attacked by any fresh air or sunshine at all. She had made an exception to the rule once, and gone on holiday to Greece with Dennis, her former husband, thinking that it was just the English murky and grey version of the outside that she was adverse to. However, following a week of enduring persistent flies, noisy mosquitoes, blotchy skin, and a blocked toilet because she'd refused to put loo-paper in the small bin in the bathroom, any last hope of curing her phobia had been irrevocably destroyed. Her distaste for the 'outside' had since led her aversion to encompass 'abroad' as well. In Natalie's enclosed world, electricity (for TV, multiple hair appliances, and cooking aids), heating, air-con, make-up, drinkable water from the tap, and proper food (English chips, roasts, pies, etc.) were non-negotiable essentials. In the last twenty-four hours she had added speaking English to the list, as well as driving on the correct side of the road, and following any known road rules, which included not using every petrol station on the corner of a junction as a high-speed short cut every time the lights were on red. This perspective on minimum standards was all explained with considerable enthusiasm and passion to Vince several times before the hotel room cooled sufficiently for the exhausted Natalie to finally collapse into a deep, jet-lag induced slumber.

* * *

Following a slightly difficult night, Vince stepped out into the early morning sunshine and took in the vibrancy and chaotic bustle of the street outside. As his new world drew him in and ignited a sense of adventure and possibility, Natalie's anxieties became a distant memory. It was his first morning in the foreign metropolis and Vince was up with the birds, and ready to launch himself into his new life. The jet-lag was also partly responsible for his early start, but despite that, after all the travel over the previous days, he was keen to see a bit more of where he'd arrived. Vince had dressed cautiously to the melodious rumblings of a gently snoring Natalie. Her mental stress of being abroad had also been compounded by her physical state. She had discovered a couple of mosquito bites when getting ready for bed the night before, and became convinced that she was about to get malaria, or something worse. Before leaving the room, Vince carefully pulled back the sheet from around her lower legs to inspect the progress of the injury. He noted that there were actually quite a number of previously unrecorded bite clusters which had gradually expanded, so that her ankles looked like the essential red-spotted scarf you need to tie in a bundle and hang on the end of a stick if you plan to run away from home with minimal luggage.

Waking up the currently peaceful Natalie to discover this development for herself would have greatly impacted on the pleasant start to the day that Vince was planning for himself. He decided to let her sleep instead.

Vince had quietly closed the door behind him, so that the stressed, but now sleeping in air-con supported slumber, Natalie could enjoy a lie-in. As he ventured out into the Khoyleng morning he was delighted to find a nearby touristy café that was able to provide a fry-up breakfast. He'd already checked to see if his nan had wanted to come for breakfast, but she'd not answered her door and he assumed that she was already out and about exploring her new environs for herself. In the UK, his nan generally linked her waking hours to the annual solar rhythms. In the summer she would rise with the sun and often be down the local shop by 5.30am wondering why it wasn't open. In the dark depths of winter there were some days when she didn't surface before lunchtime, and that was only to heat up a tin of alphabetti-spaghetti before crawling back under a blanket.

Having eaten what had passed as an acceptable English breakfast, Vince returned to the hotel lobby where he was due to meet a Mr. Sophal. Vince had made the link with him via the hotel receptionist, and understood that Sophal was a kind of local estate agent.

In reality, whilst the core ability to identify a property was part of his skill-set, the business model pursued by Mr. Sophal differed greatly to that of a UK-style estate agent. The standard estate agent practice in Britain was to have a window full of adverts displaying properties to buy or rent. People could then peer through the window, study the photo that had been taken at a strange angle to make everything look twice as big than it actually was, and then decide whether to pursue their interest in this deception further. This would lead to a conversation within the establishment with a person whose job it was to help sell properties at the highest price, and not with a person that wanted to support anxious people desperately needing somewhere to live and make a well-balanced decision about their life-changing investment. Once in the shop, the agent then further embellished the deception that the photo initiated, by avoiding any details that might suggest the ownership of the property was going to involve structurally underpinning the building, rebuilding the decaying sewage system, or replacing all the timber that was struggling to hold up the roof. In fact, any information which might have been useful to help you avoid being taken to court and sued by the local council for being in possession of a structurally unsafe building and hazard to public safety, once your ownership had become official.

Mr. Sophal, in contrast, was an agent to whom you described the sort of thing you were looking for and where you think you might find it. He would then head out into the metropolis to investigate potential properties on your behalf. This involved a process of meeting established landlords who had properties to rent, and spotting any other buildings that were neither for sale nor for rent, but fitted the given description. For the latter, his role was to then persuade the owners that they'd be better off if they moved in with their sister's family down the road and to let the property to some cashed-up foreigners for a couple of years and use the money to secure a loan for a new SUV.

Mr. Sophal arrived at the reception of the hotel. The receptionist then called Vince over from where he was lounging in a wicker chair, enjoying his view of the street life. Vince was reassured to find that Sophal's English was more than up to the job in hand. Vince spent a long time explaining to Mr. Sophal what sort of place he was looking for in the new guesthouse. He'd given this quite a lot of thought and come up with a list of un-negotiable essentials. Firstly, the property had to be in a prime location and should be near something touristy. It should be within easy walking distance of a popular monument or museum, and have at least one western-style food restaurant located nearby. The building should have the options for ten or twelve en-suite double rooms, a kitchen, a breakfast area, and a reception. In addition there needed to be living quarters for him and the family. To Vince, it seemed like this initial list of criteria would provide a good set up to start with. Having limited experience in actually managing a guesthouse, particularly in a foreign country, it would be better to walk before he could run. Therefore, despite Fairchild's significant budget and overwhelming enthusiasm to spend it flamboyantly, taking on a fifty room hotel was not on the agenda just yet.

Mr. Sophal listened attentively to Vince's description of his dream property, and made some notes. He didn't think that there were any ready-made guesthouses around where the owners were looking for someone to lease. However, he knew a few places that might be appropriate for a quick conversion. He went on to explain to Vince that in the country of Feiquon, setting up a new guesthouse or restaurant was almost as easy as taking over an existing one. You didn't have the government restrictions like they had in the West. He would check out the availability of suitable buildings that morning, and agreed to meet with Vince in the afternoon so that he could take him to see some of the best choices. Vince watched as Mr. Sophal disappeared enthusiastically down the street on his moped. As he did so, Vince's nan came into view on the opposite side of the street and crossed the road to come and join Vince.

"Mornin' Nan. You been up long?"

"I've been having noodles in the market down the end of the street, Vince. They're a bit like spaghetti hoops, but longer, and without the tomato sauce. They've got proper butchers in there, Vince. It's a proper market like the old days before the pissin' supermarkets put everything in cling-film and made all the food taste of plastic. Yaw can get fresh offal, chickens' feet, cow hooves…everything. Back in my day, I'd be glad to get hold of a good hoof and brew up a nice soup on the fire for when you grand-dad got back from work. Nowadays soups are all tarted-up fancy French sounding nonsense and pissin' croutons."

"I'm going up to check on Nat. We all have to meet back down here at 2.00pm so that we can go with the estate agent bloke to look at properties for the guesthouse. Make sure you're ready, Nan."

"Mind you Vince, they did have some live frogs in the market, so you'll need to keep your pissin' guard up or you'll find they're serving you up sommat foreign."

Vince paused for a moment to digest the idea that despite being explorers in the mystic orient his nan's definition of 'foreign' was still primarily limited to her blinkered view of the French nation and their marginally different culture to her own. He chose to remind himself that they'd agreed Natalie would be in charge of catering decisions, rather than his nan. It was a memory from which he gleaned a certain sense of reassurance.

Property

Three in a rattling tuk-tuk, they pelted down one of the main drags, weaving in and out of cars, cyclos and petrol stations as they went. Vince was regretting their choice of tuk-tuk driver, having hoped for someone more sedate in light of his girlfriend's stress-induced tirade about local transportation the previous evening. Natalie had risen for lunch, but was still not in the best of moods. On waking, she too had observed that the extent of the mosquito plague manifesting on her lower limbs had been underestimated the night before, and the swollen bite marks littering her sensitive skin were far more prevalent than had previously been realised. This had meant that in order to make a public appearance she'd been forced to wear long socks to protect her legs, an inelegant look which then didn't go with the shoes. Vince knew from experience that once the shoes were wrong, the day could only go downhill from there on.

As they scooted through traffic, Vince held Natalie's hand in what he hoped would be a soothing and reassuring way. Meanwhile the tuk-tuk rattled onwards, following its random haphazard route. On the rare occasion that they stopped at a traffic light, Vince was surprised to see how few vehicles pulled up around them. In the mad sprint to get to the lights it felt like they were vying for position with at least a hundred other road users, and yet when they all paused for breath, he could see there were only about twenty other vehicles at most, and the majority of them were mopeds.

The tuk-tuk driver had received clear instructions from Mr. Sophal to follow his moped to the first guesthouse option. Natalie was extremely concerned that Sophal had sped away out of sight, which would mean they would be lost and without the language skills to become found again. The tuk-tuk driver wasn't too bothered by Sophal's enthusiasm for racing ahead. Neither was Vince, as he knew that Mr. Sophal wouldn't get paid if he lost them.

Sophal's job was completely contrary to the needs of his clients. His primary concern was to find the most expensive property that he could. After all, he was not being paid by the hour. The usual deal between the agent and property owner is that the agent who finds the leaser gets the first month's rent for doing so. Therefore, the higher the rent, the bigger the wad of notes that Sophal would be able to cram into his back pocket, and he could then head out to a karaoke bar. For this reason, it was quite difficult for someone to find a reasonably priced place to live using this method of estate agenting. The agent was only after places with a high rent, and the renters put up the rent to cover the month for which they had to pay the agent. Luckily for Vince, Jonathan Fairchild was his benefactor, and he would be picking up all the bills, regardless of Vince's shortcomings in negotiation skills and Sophal's honed skills in his.

Eventually, the tuk-tuk driver pulled off the busy road and into a more residential area, where he slowly drew up next to Mr. Sophal's moto. Sophal had already dismounted from his motorbike, and had the owner of the building lined up with the keys ready in his hands so that he could unlock the padlock on the large iron gates.

"This is the best place, I think. It has everything you asked for, Mr. Vince."

Mr. Sophal motioned to a tall but remarkably thin, modern-looking building. It wasn't at all what Vince had imagined. He therefore struggled to equate it with Sophal's confident stance on being the best place with everything. However, Vince realised he probably wasn't too sure what it was that he had imagined. This was a thin, five storey building, snuggly slotted into place in the middle of a narrow street. Vince studied it for while, wondering if it really was the best place for a touristy guesthouse, and why that would be the case. Having drawn a blank on this demanding query, in his brief pause of contemplation he decided it might be worth asking instead.

"Am yaw sure, Mr. Sophal? What is it that makes you think this is the best place for us to set up a guesthouse?"

"Mr. Vince. It has everything. Reception area, twelve rooms, many with options for bathrooms, it's near to the tourist and prawn market, which sells silk, clothes and tourist things, just three streets' short walk that way."

Deciding it was time to move the real estate process up a notch, Mr. Sophal motioned them to step through the gateway and inside the building, followed by the silent but respectful landlord, Mr. Piseth.

With the relief that had accompanied the end of the tortuous tuk-tuk ride, Natalie's stress levels seemed to be decreasing a little. Despite a resultant slight increase in her capacity to retain emotional balance, her jet-lag immediately picked up again. Vince was pleased to note that she was returning from 'thunderous and argumentative' back to 'disgruntled and sleepy'. He reckoned if he could find somewhere for her to sit just inside the front door, he and his nan could explore the rest of the property without having to be sensitive to her delicate state.

The building did, indeed, show promise, and had possibly been built with the option of being a guesthouse in mind. However, it was a new structure, and as a result a lot of the rooms hadn't been quite finished. They lacked things like electricity and plumbing. There were two to three potential guest rooms on each of the five floors, and the promise of developing a breakfast area and garden on the flat rooftop.

Vince and his nan busily inspected each room. Vince tried to be professional and made notes of the more obvious changes and upgrades that the rooms needed in order to make them habitable. His nan, meanwhile, went round violently kicking at doors and pulling on wires to test their durability. No doubt her fears for the quality of foreign furnishing in Mrs. Reynolds' house had remained at the forefront of her concerns and she didn't want them to make the same mistake.

The steps to the top of the building were steep, but eventually they arrived on the roof.

"How do you find the view, Mr. Vince? It is very good, no?"

"It's very nice, Mr. Sophal. Where exactly are we in terms of the tourist areas and the centre of the city? Are there many guesthouses in this part of town?"

"Mr Vince, this is the most popular, upcoming part of the capital. The tourists like to walk in the street, experience the culture, and buy cheap copies of clothes and DVDs in the markets."

The mention of markets seemed to reignite some enthusiasm from Vince's nan.

"Well there had better be some good butchers in these markets of yours as well. Not just this tourist tat. I've not come all the way to Asia to eat cuts of meat that taste like pissin' plastic. I had a pork chop from the supermarket last week that would have been better as a pissin' door stop than a meal."

Vince had already suffered one butcher based conversation earlier in the day. Having realised this was something his nan needed to get out of her system, he chose not to intervene while she accosted Mr. Sophal for more information.

"And what about frogs? Are they doing frogs at these pissin' markets? What if someone knocks over the frog-bucket and before you know it there are pissin' frogs all over the fruit and veg?"

Sophal was able to point in different directions to at least three markets and explain why different tourists liked each one, as well as providing a review of the butchery potential and the range of meat products that would probably be on offer. This gave Vince some breathing space to develop questions that would address slightly more practical concerns.

"Parking could be a bit of a problem, Mr. Sophal. I notice that there is no room on the street. There isn't even a proper pavement. Where do people put their cars?"

"Nobody comes to be a tourist in Khoyleng with a car. They take a flight, and then they take a tuk-tuk. If you have a moto you keep in the reception at night when you lock up."

Mr. Sophal had a good answer for everything, and there were certainly pros as well as cons to renting the place. The rooms needed a lot of work, but they had potential. Vince would need to negotiate with the landlord to see how the costs for these improvements could be shared. There was no parking, but there was a nice roof garden that could be developed into something a bit special. There was also access to local tourist markets, which ticked one of the boxes from Vince's original criteria. Vince leaned on the wall that encircled the flat roof and gazed out at the sprawl of Khoyleng while he thought about his next move. Clearly they needed to see some of the other options for guesthouses that Mr. Sophal had scouted for them so that they could make comparisons. He also realised that he needed to find out a lot more about the city itself. It was becoming clear that he didn't know what the tourist attractions were, or the layout of the place, so it was impossible to judge if this was a good location or not.

As Vince was in deep thought, Natalie arrived noisily up the stairs, perspiring heavily and with laboured breathing as she tried to catch her breath. Clearly being abandoned alone on the ground floor was less preferable to making the effort to see what was going on without her. She joined Vince and his nan and leaned over the roof garden wall to study the view.

"That's a bloomin' hell of a lot of stairs, Vince. What's the mosquito situation like up here?"

Natalie took a very deep breath in the hope it would cure her of her breathlessness. It didn't work. It just made the subsequent ones even more rapid as her lungs tried to return to their original rhythm. Away from the noise of the streets below, the sound of her panting was like that of an out of shape St. Bernard having dragged a distressed family of climbers off an alp, and then as an after-thought pulled them up five flights of stairs so they could see the view.

Mr. Sophal took the opportunity to interject:

"No problem up here for mosquitos, Mrs. Vince. Mosquitos are very bad fliers. They don't go so high, which means you wouldn't find them up here on the roof."

Natalie took another very deep breath.

"Well let's bloomin'-well take it then."

The document man

The job of Mr. Vanarith was to understand the system. Once you understood how the system worked in Feiquon, anything was possible. Luckily for Mr. Vanarith, he was one of the few who did. He had lived and worked in the Laeket district of town for the past thirty years. He had started off as a teacher at a secondary school. However, due to his language skills in French, Chinese and basic Russian, he had been reassigned to do clerical work in the local government. During that time he had studied some English at an evening class, and managed to get quite a good job at the post office in the 'Estranger' section of the mail sorting office. After a few years he was transferred back to the government under the Ministry of Foreign Affairs. It was here that he combined his intelligence, skills and good fortune to be able to understand an administrative system that few others had completely grasped. In his retirement, he now worked freelance as the document man.

It could be argued that the current bureaucracy had evolved at a time of limited national wealth and had led to a need for government employees on minimal unliveable salaries to seek out options to supplement their incomes to feed their families. The market forces of supply and demand were applied, which dictated that when supplying a good or service you extracted the market price from the buyer. For government employees on minimal salaries, their commodity in the marketplace was documentation. Unless a document was signed and stamped by the correct people in the right order then it had no value, and the person who needed it as proof of permission or a right to proceed could no longer advance themselves as they required. Consequently, the laws for supply and demand were applied through bureaucracy. Therefore, if you wanted to have a driving licence, you did not take a driving test; you bought your licence, regardless of your capacity to control a motor vehicle. If children wanted to pass their exams, their families bought their certificates; their ability to excel in the subject being quite irrelevant. As time passed, this system of valuing the physical document rather than what ability the content should have represented became entrenched and normalised.

To start a restaurant or hotel in Feiquon, the necessity for vast reams of paperwork from every government department imaginable was inevitable. A bureaucracy would often require the hotelier to have a licence to trade, a licence to serve alcohol, a licence to sell food, planning permission to convert a building to be suitable to house overnight guests, parking permits, documents showing you met loading and unloading regulations, kitchens certified by health inspectors, electrical installations certified by the authorities. In Feiquon this was magnified by the need to do this in a way that satisfied the village authorities as well as the district, city and provincial authorities, and also the local police force. Of course, if you were either serving in the local government or a senior member of the police force then the rules were more relaxed. Unfortunately Vince didn't fall within this category.

The need to pay everyone for a different document to enable you to get to the next document and to ensure everyone along the bureaucratic chain had no cause for complaint was where Mr. Vanarith came in. As would be the case with an Olympic judge in a filled auditorium watching the gymnastic ribbon-twirling section, Mr. Vanarith was one of the few people who could observe the delicate nuances, and either understand or care about the subtleties of what was going on. For a fee, his job was to go around to all of the different offices and fill in all of the paperwork, ensuring that the appropriate fees had been accounted for, and deliver it all back to the business owner. After that, the client would be free to get on with the business of making profit, safe in the knowledge that the police and anyone else in authority were already more than content with their recent arrival in the neighbourhood.

Mr. Sophal had asked Mr. Piseth, the landlord, to bring Mr. Vanarith to the building for an introduction, knowing that if Vince didn't suss out the administration of how to get started, then he wouldn't rent, and Mr. Sophal would miss out on his payment. Mr. Sophal oversaw the proceedings, while Mr. Vanarith explained the considerable list of official documents that they needed to get hold of, how much each one would cost, and the additional fee that he required for providing his service.

Vince listened to what the document man had to say.

"I see why we need the licences and that. I don't get why we're paying the police though."

Mr. Sophal decided to answer for Mr. Vanarith:

"Mr Vince, it is important that the police know you and can see that you are a good person. Otherwise they will get suspicious of you and when you have a problem like a thief breaking in, then they might be less interested to help."

"I guess it's a bit like the Mafia in the movies, with their protection rackets and that? Only not quite the same. Like those Chinese ones in the films, perhaps?"

Despite watching a lot of B-movies throughout his upbringing, for the moment Vince couldn't remember what the famous crime syndicate type group were called. In his mind, Vince wanted to refer to them as 'triangles' but instinctively felt this was probably the wrong word, so didn't offer it as an option. Fortunately his nan was more on the ball:

"Yam thinkin' of them triads, Vince. Back in the '60s, when I was working the big casinos in London, they were always pissin' hangin' around."

Despite his need to get down to the matter in hand, which was to set Mr. Vanarith off on his task of sourcing expensive but vital documents, Vince was intrigued. It was rare that his aging nan intrigued him, but on this occasion a new element to his nan's history had popped up which had not been part of the continual loop of memories that were usually on offer. He raised an eyebrow to signal the need for further clarification. A rarity when it came to communicating with his nan, as normally he just ignored her.

"You worked in London casinos with triads?"

"It was back in the '60s, Vince. They were always very polite. I was usually on the Blackjack, whilst my friend Sandy Drapper used to work the roulette. She then went off with some rich fella to Spain but it didn't work out, and she ended up coming back and getting a job at the cash 'n' carry. You think it's goin' be a bargain having a card to one of them places, but by the time you've bought a bulk load of stuff you didn't need, you'd have been better off spending your pissin' money at the corner shop."

The overall lack of triad information in the story reminded Vince why he didn't usually ask his nan follow-up questions. He decided to return to the discussion with Sophal and Vanarith and establish what the full extent of the document investment would be if he was to avoid all triad type situations.

Karot Lu Goccelu Yak

Within a few days of his arrival in Feiquon, Vince was renting the building that would become his guesthouse, and was ready to start setting up the intricacies of his business. Coming up with a good and original name for a guesthouse can be very tricky, so Vince and Natalie had therefore decided not to bother, and to use the one they already had. According to the receptionist at the hotel where they'd been staying since their arrival in Khoyleng, the 'Karot Lu Goccelu Yak', was as close to 'the Carrot and Jam Kettle' as it is possible to get, without the receptionist actually understanding what a jam kettle was.

Vince wasn't too sure himself. It is often the case that you fail to question things that you took on in faith from a young age. It is only when you have to explain it to someone else that you realise you're not as confident about the whole thing as you should be. A good example of this phenomena was when Vince had spotted large green things outside of the markets and had the gradual realisation that these were actually coconuts. Not some type of special Feiquon coconut either, but the standard international type. Up until this point, Vince had understood that the small brown hairy coconuts at fairgrounds, being the same things that fell from trees and broke in half on Bounty adverts, were coconuts in their entirety, and not just their inner shell. Until you are forced to question a long held belief, it's surprising what incomplete truths you find that you've been inadvertently holding on to.

For the guesthouse naming dilemma, Vince had called on his nan to provide everyone with a definition of a jam kettle. Natalie, the receptionist and he then received a lengthy and insightful explanation, where they all learned about the necessity of borrowing copperware from Mrs. Teasley during the war, who was in the next street after the undertakers, which "is now a pissin' chemist". 'Making jam' and 'there being a war on', it seemed were inextricably linked in those days. By the time the problems with Mr. Brathwaite's apple and pear orchards, the main local source of fruit for jam, had been added to the mix (the orchard being commandeered by the free-French, which brought into question of whether they'd be rationed because, whilst the free French weren't civilians, they weren't the British army either), Vince was actually even less sure that he knew what a jam kettle was. However, a possible interpretation in Feiquon for 'Carrot and Pot-Jam' was eventually eked out from the confusion. Vince realised this was probably as close as they were going to get, and they decided to go with it.

Sophea

Sophea applied for the job of receptionist at the 'Karot Lu Goccelu Yak' having seen a flyer glued on to a metal pole for electric cables at the end of her street. The very fact that she was prepared to go close enough to this particular over-burdened electrocution hazard to read the notice was already a significant demonstration of the courage she was prepared to call upon in her determination to search for employment.

As with many young go-getters in the 'burbs of Khoyleng, she applied for nearly all the jobs that were advertised, regardless of what they were or whether or not she was remotely qualified. For this purpose she had a cover letter that a man who helps people to write cover letters had written, and a CV prepared in a similar one-size-fits-all way. She had then mass produced these documents at the nearby photocopy shop. As with her numerous peers, she dropped them off every time an advert for a job ventured forth. The high volume of job seekers therefore very much influenced the job-seeking market. Employers were forced to wade through hundreds of generic, un-targeted applications that were in no way prepared for the job for which they'd been submitted. However, as is the experience for some patrons of the national lottery in the UK, who put down the same numbers week in, week out just in case, occasionally the CV lottery paid off and an application, by chance, vaguely matched the job in question.

Vince had never interviewed anyone before. Also, he had yet to work out how the CV lottery worked. As a result, he was studying each of the many CVs that he'd received with far more attention than some of them perhaps deserved. His original plan to narrow down the field was firstly to find any that were in English, with the assumption that the applicant would have good English skills. By doing this he failed to question his assumption that all the applicants had written their own CVs. The second filter was to pick ones with experience in hotel management. The first round of CV examination had left him with about ninety CVs, and the second filtering left him with none.

As most of the ninety CVs had passport photos of the

applicants stapled to the front, he'd gone for a new tack, and started picking ones that look a bit like receptionists. This had got him down to ten finalists. He was reaching the end of the finalists pile when Sophea's CV caught his eye. As with many other candidates, in her language section of her CV she had actually made a table. There were categories along the top for 'fluent', 'moderate' and 'basic'. Within the table she had then ticked 'moderate' for written and spoken English, and 'mother tongue' in the Feiquon column. This, of course, for Vince was a minimum requirement. Beneath this, however, it detailed that not only had she studied English at high school but had worked at an English teaching school whilst studying accounting. From this additional gem of information, he surmised that not only was she going to be very helpful with communication to guests and to himself, but would also be able to manage all of the guests' bills and records.

Vince called Sophea on his new mobile. A very difficult conversation then ensued, and Vince assumed that she must have had a problem with the phone at her end of the line, which explained the minimal comprehension of anything he said. Eventually he had arranged for her to come for an interview that afternoon.

Sophea was surprised to get an interview. She had almost forgotten that she'd applied for the guesthouse receptionist job. After all, she had no receptionist experience, and her basic English was shaky at best. She'd never really practised her English, and certainly hadn't talked to foreigners before. It was very different to talking with other Feiquons, trying to practise basic English using the same shared vocabulary that they had learned. Even when her uncle got her in to do the accounting at the English school that ran classes for kids early in the morning before they then went to the state schools, she would try and shut out the noise of them chanting English phrases so that she could concentrate on fiddling the books properly for the betterment of her extended family. However, a job was a job. It was better than the constant ironing that she got lumbered with by her mother, who ran a small laundry at the front of her house. Hopefully this foreigner wouldn't be from some religious organisation and make her go to church on Sundays and expunge her salary for the benefit of a supernatural being. A friend of hers had worked for such people and she was expected to put in $10 a week to the collection. Considering the girl only got paid $120 a month, this was quite a hefty tax for a deity that was presumably on more than $120 gross themselves. It was certainly not a tax that her uncle at the English school would have stood for.

The interview

"Yaw right there? Sophea is it? Come on in and take a seat."

Sophea entered the room and made a gentle bow towards Vince, whilst briefly bringing her hands together as if in prayer. Vince then reciprocated and awkwardly mimicked the reverent gesture in the spirit of being culturally sensitive. Having achieved this exchange of muted pleasantries, Vince then motioned to the second chair in the office of The Karot. Sophea nodded, smiled politely, nodded again and then sat down.

Vince decided this was a good start. She was clearly respectful and polite. These were good attributes for an aspiring receptionist. Also, unlike Natalie, Sophea was clearly not too talkative. This would be a good and complimentary element in terms of team dynamics. He knew from his experience working at the hotel in Paddington that people staying in city guesthouses didn't want to be greeted with a long review of the day's gossip, unlike the regular bar-proppers in a suburban pub. They wanted to get checked-in and up to their rooms as efficiently and yarn-free as possible.

In the time between Vince ringing Sophea and her subsequent arrival at the guesthouse, he had crafted three insightful, yet subtle interview questions with which to provide her the opportunity to impress. He decided to crack on with the first of these straight away.

"Now Sophea, in your CV it says you worked in an English school while you were studying. How long did you keep that going for, what sort of hours were you putting in?"

"I sorry. Please you say again?"

"I'm asking about this," Vince showed her the CV and pointed to where he'd underlined the part of it that was about her uncle's English school.

"The 'Ngitteap English School'."

"Yes. This school for learn English. This my uncle school."

"Right. And how many years did you work there?"

Sophea nodded, showing she had understood and appreciated the question.

"Yes. I work there when I study accounting. I study three year."

Vince was impressed. Three years teaching English was pretty impressive. She must have very good language skills. He guessed for now she was struggling to pick up his accent and that this would improve quickly once she started work.

"Very good, Sophea. Now, it says on your CV, right, that you are 'good' at 'Word' and 'Excel'."

"Yes. I can Word, and I can using to Excel."

"Did you use Excel when you were doing your accounting, like?"

"I can be using Excel."

Sophea repeated her Excel statement, nodded and smiled. In fact she was well versed with quite a number of accounting software applications. However, she'd paid for a fairly standard CV which was personalised by her name, contact number, address and three things about her. Therefore she had been left with the standard language and computer skill tables at the bottom of the page that everyone got, and so her actual skills were quite poorly represented.

"And finally, Sophea, what is your salary expectation. How much do yaw think you should be paid each month?"

Sophea smiled with an embarrassed look.

"I not say. You decide."

"No, Sophea. What sort of money do you expect to earn each month?"

"You decide. What you think."

Sophea quietly returned to her endearingly polite smile. Vince contemplated this. It was a very polite answer, albeit a little unhelpful. In his short time in Feiquon, every time that he had bought something in the local markets he'd got the impression that he was being charged at least double the going rate. He had yet to meet anyone polite enough not to extract an exorbitant amount of money from him at the first opportunity, in the knowledge he didn't have the language skills or the bartering finesse to do anything about it. The most he'd ever got was a half-dollar discount on a handbag for Natalie as he was supposedly the first paying customer of the day, so it would be lucky for the stall owner to be generous to him. With Sophea's knowledge of finance, and yet lack of personal financial ambition, clearly there was something very special about the girl.

"Well, I think it's fair to say you've got the job, Sophea. You can start tomorrow? We're setting the whole thing up for now, but hopefully we will have customers staying here in a couple of weeks' time."

Sophea accepted the position and walked out of the future 'Karot Lu Goccelu Yak', even more surprised by this outcome than she was when she'd got the unlikely news that she'd been called to the interview in the first place. So long as her new boss didn't have her ironing the clothes of the guests for hours on end then she might as well give it a try.

Getting ready

It was less than three weeks after putting down the first two months' rent as a deposit that they were ready to open the Karot Lu Goccelu Yak. Vince was impressed with just how fast Mr. Piseth the landlord could find builders and tradesmen to sort out the guest rooms once he had realised there was some extra financing available to him and, more importantly, that there'd be limited monitoring of its use. Vince had also agreed to take on two of Piseth's daughters as chamber maids, which seemed to have added to his enthusiasm to help Vince get the guesthouse up and running. Natalie even cheered-up a little once going shopping to spend Fairchild's money on furnishing twelve bedrooms and a roof garden gave her something to do within her sphere of expertise. Sophea was available for translation as well as fabric and furnishing consultation, for which Vince was equally grateful. Vince's nan had a habit of just wandering off for the day doing her own thing, which suited Vince quite nicely as well. All in all, things were moving to plan.

Once the building improvements were underway, Vince's real challenge was putting in place strategies to attract the guests. Luckily there were people in town who could help with the marketing as well, and Vince soon had an advertising company working to get The Karot some visibility on travel websites, in fliers on airport tuk-tuks, and on posters in guesthouses they knew in other touristy towns in the country. The latter was on the assumption that a number of travellers tended to arrive in town and then find somewhere to stay, not the other way round. Helping them think about that on the day of departure for Khoyleng would do no harm at all.

Vince leaned over the low wall of the roof garden and gazed at the road below. Right now it was a normal Khoyleng street with motos zipping along, scruffy dogs milling around on the pavement, and elderly women brandishing short grass brooms, sweeping clouds of dust from in front of their own houses so that it could settle in front of their neighbours' houses. Despite the current subdued inactivity, all would change by tomorrow as the first customers for The Karrot Lu Goccelu Yak would arrive. They already had bookings for three couples on their first day of opening, and who could predict what other passing trade would come their way. A sense of pride filled Vince as he gazed down at the street, thinking about what they had achieved in such a short space of time. As he looked down, he watched a man in a baseball cap wander across the street and make his way through the gates and towards reception. Vince continued to lazily survey the road below. A tuk-tuk clattered up to the junction and swung round the corner, a woman selling bread pushed her cart along, whilst a recording advertising her wares shouted out the message on her behalf. A minute or so later the man with the baseball cap had left the guesthouse, and walked a little way up the road before calling in on a neighbouring house.

Downstairs, Sophea had been working behind the reception desk as the baseball capped local had made his appearance. He had delivered to her an elaborate cream envelope with fancy gold and pink writing on it. Sophea dutifully thanked him and carefully put the envelope behind her desk.

It would be a couple of hours before Natalie was due to return from her massage and foot spa, for which she'd found a much more posh guesthouse than theirs to meet her pampering needs. In her absence, Vince decided he'd wander down to the market and look for a couple of cheap DVDs to watch. As he walked past reception, Vince recalled the visitor he seen from the roof.

"What did the man in the red hat want, Sophea? Was he looking for a room?"

"No, Mr. Vince. He from one of you neighbour in this street. He bring letter for wedding tomorrow. You and Mrs. Natalie can to go."

Sophea held up the envelope and pulled out the invitation card so Vince could appreciate the ornate and slightly kitsch contents.

"Well it is very kind of them to think of us Sophea, but I don't think we'll be able to make it. Tomorrow is our first day of business, so we'll all be working hard."

Sophea nodded, and carefully put the invitation back in the envelope, placing it neatly on a shelf behind her desk.

The truth

Telling the truth is supposedly a simple communication of factual information. However, facts are often subjective, open to judgement, and can change over time. Indeed, go back in time a few years and the truth was as much about 'faith' as it was about 'fact'.

The 'theory of truth' is therefore a complex scholarly debate for which many an informed philosopher has felt obliged to contribute their own incomprehensible sentence, and muddy the waters further. For example, 'correspondence theory' requires truth to conform to external realities; yet being objective about these realities is quite challenging. Those in favour of 'logical positivism' seem to demand the truth's verification, of which language and method is a constraint. The constructivists consider all knowledge to be culturally derived and, therefore, truth is a social construct. The pragmatists see truth with a quality to be confirmed when judged through practice. And, of course, let's not drift down the road of 'meaningful-declarative-sentence-token-uses that are truth-bearers'.

With that in mind, the failure to appreciate these acceptable variations of the truth in our day to day lives may be more a reflection of our own modern desires to simplify. Perhaps when other cultures demonstrate a more rounded appreciation of the complexity of truth, their higher philosophical achievements should be acknowledged and applauded, rather than be viewed with concern.

Philosophers aside, in practical terms, the truth is perhaps at its most helpful when it enables us to understand what is going on around us, and leads us to an informed decision of what to do about it.

As we are all now armchair truth-philosophers, it is interesting to note that in the country of Feiquon there exists a deviation of these truth theories which could be considered as 'the theory of misleading understatement'. This criterion of the truth captures many elements of those discussed above, with the added proviso that the truth should almost always be non-confrontational and difficult to spot. Whistle-blowing therefore brings a new meaning to the phase 'passive-aggressive'.

Example 1.

A member of staff sees that you have a builder doing some work for you. They recognise the builder, and then mention to you that someone they know once told them about this builder. He had done some work for that person's neighbour, and the builder and the neighbour had had a small disagreement. You nod, make an 'hmm' kind of noise to fain interest, and return to what you were previously doing, without giving this third-hand petty gossip a second thought. However, the real message to be taken away from that incidental remark, is that person telling you this is desperate that you should understand that your builder is a known alcoholic and criminal who habitually sells off most of the cement to pay for his addictions, and everyone bar you knows that any building construction he's been involved in has to be entirely rebuilt a few months later, so you'd better sort it out quickly. The small disagreement the staff member has mentioned refers to the one held at the police station, with the neighbour strongly protesting at their house being burned to the ground and the builder's limited, albeit enthusiastic, hands-on approach to electrical engineering.

Your courageous staff member will feel that they have boldly stood up, and furnished you with the truth that you need to address the issue of your forthcoming building collapse, and will say no more about it.

Delivering the truth through the medium of misleading understatement means that it can take at least six months for some conversations to become fully understood. At the close of the above scenario you will eventually find yourself staring at the pile of rubble that was once your dream home, contemplating your financial ruin. Meanwhile your mind will drift back to the stark warning from your staff member about the builder's disagreement with the neighbour, and a few 'a-ha's' will drift through the inner monologue as what was said suddenly connects with what was meant. A few more dots get connected and you recognise your error in your under appreciation of the 'misleading understatement'. The staff member that delivered the original information will feel safe in the knowledge that they did all they could, and the only person to blame in all of this is you for not heeding their warning when it was issued.

Example 2.

You have two cleaners working in your office, and you ask the administrator to take cleaner 'A' under their wing. This go-getter is always at work early, shows initiative, is keen to help with other tasks, and has been studying administration at night school. Maybe cleaner 'A' deserves an opportunity, in light of her hard work and dedication. She could start with a little bit of training on filing so that one day she might be better placed to climb the ladder and be a candidate for an office assistant position.

The administrator replies that they're not sure that cleaner 'A' would be very good, and it would be far better to choose cleaner 'B' if more help is needed in the office. You frown in the knowledge that cleaner 'B's only show of initiative was the time she remembered not to dust your computer screen with a brillo pad. You also then regret that your administrator doesn't have more initiative themselves, and decide to do the filing on your own as it will be quicker.

It's probable, assuming you've already checked that the administrator and cleaner 'B' are not related, that the administrator has some inside knowledge on cleaner 'A'. Therefore, the full extent of the truth that cleaner 'B' is a better bet, will be because cleaner 'A' is known to be either (a) pregnant, (b) about to get married to a chauvinistic idiot, so will never work again outside the confines of her own home or (c) both. The administrator has therefore decided it's not worth wasting their own time giving cleaner 'A' any further training, as they'll only have to train somebody else in a few months' time after she leaves. However, to tell you this directly would mean disclosing a truth that is not theirs to tell. To share this information would be confrontational towards cleaner 'A'.

Two months later you receive your wedding invitation letter from cleaner 'A' (which is expected to be returned with a minimum $20 bill in it whether you go or not), and later in the week at the office party you then meet the future Mr. 'A', who is clearly a chauvinistic idiot who will make sure his new wife never works outside the confines of her own home ever again. Gradually you cast your mind back to a long since forgotten conversation, and the penny drops on the 'misleading understatement' provided by the annoyingly vague and yet astute administrator.

Cultural sensitivity was never Vince's strong suit. However, with this heightened level of nuance and subtlety of information sharing and understanding the truth, Vince didn't really stand much of a chance. On this particular day, Sophea had dutifully passed on the information that their neighbour had invited them to a wedding. Sophea had given Vince full warning of it and had even opened the invitation for him so that it was abundantly clear what was about to happen. How he chose to deal with this problem was now entirely up to him.

Opening day

Early in the morning Vince, Natalie, Vince's nan and Sophea all went to the market to stock up on fresh food. The newly constructed bar on the roof garden was already fully stocked with beverages, but Natalie was determined that freshly cooked food with a choice for English cuisine was the key to their dining success. They returned on foot from their morning's shopping weighed down with heavy plastic bags filled with vegetables, meat and fresh fruit. As they turned the corner and started down their small road towards the guesthouse they notice a few tables and chairs were being set up at the side of the street.

Vince pointed out the unusual development to Natalie by swinging a vegetable-filled plastic bag towards the activity.

"Must be for that wedding, Nat."

"What bloomin' wedding? I never heard about a wedding."

"We got an invite yesterday afternoon, but we're too busy to go and join in, as it's our first day opening. I didn't think you'd want to accept."

"Vince, what are you like? Yawm supposed to at least reply to a wedding invitation so they know what numbers to expect and that. Have we still got the invite?"

Sophea took the opportunity to defuse the situation.

"I have the letter in my desk. It polite to put twenty dollars each in envelope as gift and send back. I can do for you if you think it's good."

"I think you should Sophea – get the money from Vince once he's put the bags in the kitchen. Honestly Vince, you drag us out here to this mosquito-filled hell, and now you're upsetting the neighbours 'n all."

Having given Sophea forty bucks to stuff into the wedding envelope, Vince went round the guesthouse, checking all the rooms for the umpteenth time to make sure they were definitely ready for the grand opening. He then ascended to the roof garden to clean and recheck the bar. Natalie had returned to her kitchen where she was mass producing steak-and-ale pies and lasagne.

Vince looked up suddenly from the bar, pulled from his peaceful daydream about the exciting arrival of the first guests. The advent of incredibly loud, distorted music coming from the street below was the reason for his startled reaction. He left the bar area and leaned over the roof garden wall to see if he could locate and understand the full extent of the phenomena.

Feiquon Weddings

The slightly leaky function room at the back of a run-down pub is not a feature of Khoyleng suburbia, and therefore limits the options available for socially charged gatherings. Consequently, if your daughter is getting married it's not uncommon to have the reception in the street outside at the front of your house. The other big difference between weddings in distant exotic landscapes and the types that Vince was aware of from his Midlands environment is the finances. Couples where Vince came from might save for a few years to get the funds together for their dream wedding, having previously spent several years scraping together the deposit for a dilapidated semi or small terraced house in which to cultivate a forthcoming brood. However, in this Feiquon scenario, it was actually possible to get things happening quickly, and even make quite a bit of cash. The starting rate to attend a wedding reception in the capital was twenty dollars a head, with the cash to be returned in your invitation letter as a wedding gift. However, if the family of the wedding party had previously attended the wedding of one of the guests, then that guest would be expected to put more in their envelope than the amount they received at their wedding. Failure to do so would result in considerable loss of face, and as a result most couples would record in detail the gifted amounts from their guests to make sure they could exceed them at future weddings, and thus avoid embarrassment. This system could backfire if one of your guests was due for a wedding in the near future as they could then put in a larger amount than the standard $20 for your gift, knowing it would come back again quite soon and with interest. On this basis then, it was a good idea to invite as many people to your wedding as you possibly could, preferably skewing the demographics towards people whose wedding you'd already gone to or those who were already married but didn't have children aged about eight or upwards, who might themselves get married in the next ten years. Vince and Natalie were excellent choices as guests on this basis, as it was pretty much a guaranteed one-way flow of spondulicks.

Once the guest list is finalised and invites are issued, the family then hires a large truckload of tables and chairs, puts up an array of awnings and tents in the middle of the street and pay the police to stop all traffic whilst keeping them occupied with free food and beer. If the police fail to close the road then the fact that there is now a mobile kitchen system at one end of the street and a wall of enormous speakers at the other, solves the problem anyway. As the party set-up is being rented by the day, the suppliers are expected to arrive fairly early so the customer gets their money's worth. Therefore, by the middle of the morning everything is ready to go, the sound system is blasting plinkitty-plonky xylophone music at a rate that's blowing the speakers, and shaking the glassware through the neighbours' houses. On hearing this, various elderly relatives are then inspired to start sitting at tables in their traditional dress, waiting for the monks to show up, looking bored and getting slightly sozzled with the resident policemen as there's not much else to do.

This was pretty much the stage proceedings had reached as Vince leaned over the roof garden wall to investigate the ear-wrenching assault on his peaceful potterings.

Within moments Natalie was at his side.

"What the bloomin' hell?!"

"Must be the wedding, Nat. I'd no idea it would be like this. Hopefully they'll have their lunch and then pack up so we're not disturbed by the noise."

"Stuff their bloomin' lunch, Vince! This lot look like they've moved in for the bloomin' duration. Our guests aren't going to stand for this, Vince! That is if they manage to negotiate the soup kitchen and can get to the bloomin' guesthouse in the first place! What are we doing here, Vince? It's hot, it's sweaty, my legs look like they've got the bloomin' plague. I probably have got the bloomin' plague, or at least malaria or one of those flesh-eating things, and now our business is being totally ruined by this bloomin' circus. My lasagne will be utterly ruined. Who's gonna eat it, Vince? Who? This isn't the UK. You can't just stuff it in the processor once it's started looking a bit ropey and then put it on the specials board as minestrone soup. I knew we never should have come to this bloomin' disease-infested place!"

Natalie stormed off and left Vince to ponder this many faceted situation. Could lasagne really be processed into minestrone? What percentage of commercially available minestrone was actually out-of-date lasagne that had been shoved in a blender? As he gazed at the table-filled awnings packed with elderly people and the constabulary getting communally sozzled, Vince noticed that one of the participants was his own grandmother.

Vince listened as the door to their room slammed shut behind a distraught Natalie on the floor below. Before approaching Natalie, he decided it was better to become armed with some facts about the current situation, rather than try to comfort her with ones he'd have to make up. To do this it would be best to go to reception and find out the cultural details of street weddings from Sophea. This took a while, due to the challenges of Sophea's continued inability to adapt her documented English skills to Vince's foreign accent, combined with the fact that it can be quite difficult for anyone, foreign or local, to know what's going on at a wedding anyway. Vince eventually understood that from about four in the morning the bride would have been up, getting her make-up and numerous outfits ready. The day would be peppered with visits to the monks, photo sessions with the husband and wedding party, more monk stuff, the occasional speech from the best man, more photos of the bride and groom posing with bowls of fruit, and further gifts to monks. However, what would be a safe bet was the four to five course meal in the evening, at which people would try to recoup the value of their $20 minimum gift investment by drinking far too much beer, and then the dancing in a circle to out-of-tune karaoke.

Despite being unclear on a few of the details, it was increasingly apparent that today was not the best day for The Karot to start embracing the arrival of valued guests. Two of the three bookings had given contact numbers, and so Vince phoned them, explained the problem, and suggested they look elsewhere. If the third one turned up then he'd offer to find them a different guesthouse and put them in a tuk-tuk.

Armed with a cultural understanding of proverbial knot-tying that was now at a similar level of clarity and understanding to anyone else on the street, it was time to update and try to console Natalie. Vince entered their room and found her sulking on the bed, picking at the scabs on her legs left by the mosquito bites.

"Looks like you were right, Nat, it could go on all evening, according to Sophea. I've rung up the guests and cancelled their bookings so they don't arrive and get disappointed. We'll probably have more bookings again by the weekend."

There was a long pause and no response from Natalie. Clearly his efforts to solve the guest issue were insufficient to raise her spirits. It was time for a different tack.

"Well, it's nearly lunchtime. Why don't we make a start on that lasagne?"

Prawns

A large serving of home-made lasagne and a couple of shots of Malibu had helped bring Natalie round a bit. Her focus had shifted from the financial ruin linked to the loss of first night guests, to the financial ruin linked to the $40 they'd had to pay to entitle them to lose the guests in the first place. Not only was Natalie an emotional lady, but she was also something of a miser, and the latter did tend to dominate her decision-making processes in the longer term. The only way to save anything from this disaster-filled day was to follow the example of all the other invitees of the wedding, and try to get their money's worth at the buffet, or whatever it was, before they were too drunk to claw back some of their investment.

By early evening, and a few more shots of Malibu, Vince and Natalie both changed into something a bit more formal, and started to wander down to join the other guests in the street. Vince had found himself a fresh shirt to put on, and Natalie had thrown caution to the wind and slipped into her black, strappy cocktail dress, which was the only dressy outfit she'd packed. A lot of her luggage had been beach wear, as this fitted with her pre-departure vision of 'abroad', although much of her wardrobe had since been deemed largely impractical. A large dollop of foundation was spread over her scab infested legs, like she was icing a particularly sickly cake, and it was time to head out.

Having gently bowed in a non-committal apologetic sort of way at various wedding guests, they made their way over to the table where Vince's nan had established residency since late morning.

"Yaw right, Nan? Yaw seem to be enjoying yourself."

Vince's Nan looked up from her conversation with one of the guests. Her eyes had the inevitable glaze that accompanies an afternoon of drinking beer outside on a hot day.

"What yaw doing dressed all in black, Natalie? This is a pissin' wedding not a pissin' funeral!"

"It's a bloomin' cocktail dress, Nan. And I'm dressed appropriately, as I'm not trying to either outdo the bride or get off with the best man. Anyway, look at you in your bloomin' flowery dress from the '70s. You should watch out that you don't get swarmed by a load of bees on the look-out for pollen!"

Vince realised that, despite her attendance at the wedding, Natalie was still a little upset by the event's existence, and this was very much amplified by the afternoon's visit to the Malibu bottle. He decided to steer the conversation away from the sartorial, and motioned towards the man seated next to his florally shrouded grandmother.

"I see you've met up with Mr. Vanarith, Nan. Yaw right there, Mr. Vanarith? How's the document business going?"

"Hello, Mr. Vince. I am good. Have some beer! Cheers!"

Vince was immediately provided with a small glass into which beer from a can was added. This was quickly followed by numerous large ice cubes, dropped in from sufficient height so that most of the beer spilled out on to the metal foldaway table and soaked into the white table cloth that covered it.

"Cheers, Mr. Vanarith."

Following Vanarith's lead, Vince downed the beer that remained in his glass, so that Vanarith could refill both glasses ready for the next 'cheers'. Natalie had already poured herself a beer in a slightly larger glass, but without the ice, and followed suit with a down-in-one. The beers and cheers started to flow with the monotony of a golfing enthusiast steering every conversation to become a monologue about golf. Indeed, similar to that of any enthusiast using their chosen interest to blot-out their own real-life monotony. Fortunately for Vince, Mr. Vanarith was piling ice cubes into his glass, which were melting rapidly in the warm beer, so that the rate at which Vince could get drunk was never going to overtake the rate at which the added water was sobering him up. Natalie was beyond the reach of Vanarith and his large ice bucket and so did not suffer the same problem. By the fourth ice-filled 'cheers', a waitress brought out a course of food to the table. Other tables were already ahead of their group by a few courses. Vince couldn't help but notice one of the servers was the landlord's elder daughter, who was actually supposed to be working at The Karot that evening. Obviously there wasn't much work to be doing right now in his besieged guesthouse, but he suspected that this moonlighting had been planned some way in advance of his decision to cancel the bookings.

The second course of food to arrive, following several more glasses of beer, downed-in-one to ever enthusiastic chants of 'cheers', was a seafood salad.

"You must eat the prawns. They are very good."

Mr. Vanarith helped himself to a crustacean from the plate in the centre of their small table. He then started to place a few onto Vince's nan's plate before starting to show her how to use chop sticks. If Vince didn't know any better he'd swear that Vanarith was flirting with his nan. Also, as he did know better, he could see that his nan was flirting back.

"Yaw right there, Nat?"

Vince leaned over to his partner to enquire about her wellbeing, and in doing so became aware of her absence. Assuming she'd gone to find a toilet he turned back to observe the chopstick lesson.

"Chuck us that prawn there Mr. Vanarith, and I'll give it another go with these pissin' sticks of yours."

"These prawns are from the sea, brought from the coast this morning, but we also have very good river prawns that they can catch in the rivers and lakes of Feiquon."

"Yaw can get prawns like this in the freezer section down at the co-op, but they're a lot more pink than these, and they don't have the legs on them. I never get them as they'm too expensive on my pension, but Mrs. Garret once did prawn cocktails at a barbecue, and Mr. Harris, who does the painting and decorating, got pissin' food poisoning from it."

"They catch them off the shore with special nets that go along the sea at the bottom."

"Mr. Harris offered to do my skirting boards and round the door frames once. And it seemed like a good idea until he told me how much he'd charge. I said I'd pissin' well do it myself for that price. Got Vince to do it in the end."

"You need to hold the chopstick a bit lower down. That's better."

"Probably lucky for him that he got that food poisoning. Any excuse to get out of staying too long at a do round at Mrs. Garret's."

Vince's attention was suddenly drawn away from the fascinating cross cultural comparison of the social influence of prawns. As he watched the serving girl remove the half empty plate of prawn and replace it with a rice-based dish, he spotted a distant Natalie in the midst of several guests dancing in the street beyond where the tables were set up.

In the absence of stimulating and erudite conversation, he thought he might as well go and join her.

Dancing

The traditional dance on these occasions requires a male and female to politely partner-up and follow similar pairings to promenade in an anticlockwise circle. The women will do elegant and flowing swoops with their arms, lifting and raising their hands and spreading their fingers at an appropriate moment to symbolise the traditional dispersal of rice seeds onto fresh paddy. The men, meanwhile, shuffle along to the side of this display of elegance, with a range of moves correlated to their degree of shyness, degree of beer in-take, and degree to which they want to impress the girl next to them.

Natalie was in the midst of this, doing the Malibu-induced version of rice planting, which probably wouldn't result in a particularly good harvest. Vince stepped in beside her and did the shy flat-footed version of what the bloke in front of him was doing. Fortunately, the pairing in front included Sophea his receptionist, so Vince felt advice could be at hand if the dance got any more elaborate. As the song finished, Vince looked at Natalie. Despite her sweaty face, she did at least look like she was finally cheering up a bit. Perhaps, rather than a disastrous first night at The Karot, it could actually be a turning point where their new life and cultural shift was embraced, rather than seen as a terrible insect-dominated imposition. As these positive thoughts drifted happily through Vince's mind and mixed delicately with the ice-cube diluted beer, there was a squeal of feedback from the speakers followed by a loud announcement from somewhere on the other side of the dinner tent. The Feiquon announcement was then followed by one in English from an elderly but rather pissed-up female guest.

"Me an' Mr. Vanarith am gonna do 'YMCA' on the karaoke. Get up and get ready to dance, it's a pissin' good tune, this one."

Natalie grabbed Vince with one arm and Sophea with another.

"I bloomin' love this song. My chance to show this lot how to dance properly!"

Natalie's enthusiasm might have been tempered had she

fully registered that it was Vince's nan and an elderly Feiquon gentleman who were about to enthral them with this modern-day un-rehearsed rendition. However, she was having fun so why spoil it?

"Now, get your pissin' hands in the air. Here we go!...*Young man, there's naw need to feel daw'n,*"

"*I say, young men, pick – you – sell – off – groun',*"

"*I said young man, cos yaw'm in a new town...*"

By this stage Vince was doing his best to remember what the actions were. Dancing in front of a mirror to the village people wasn't something he had spent his youth obsessing over. Natalie, meanwhile, was in a whirl of arm actions and confused guests.

Her first reaction had been to prevent Sophea from making a discrete exit and try to get her following the actions. She then grabbed the lad who was trying to impress Sophea and got him involved as well. Seemingly, he decided that going along with the mad foreigner would help out Sophea, and therefore improve his chances of making a good impression on her.

"*...It's fun to stay at the Y...M...C A...*"

As per the dance requirements Natalie had her arms up in the air in a 'Y' shape and was encouraging those around her to do the same.

"Look Vince – we've finally put a bit of spark into this party. Look at them. They've never had so much fun!"

Natalie pointed at a group of young men who were all laughing drunkenly at her antics.

"Miss Natalie, please, you should stop now!"

Sophea was tugging at Natalie, trying desperately to get her to sit down."

"Bloomin' hell, Sophea!"

"Miss Natalie! You embarrass. They not have fun. They laugh at you. Laugh at your under-arm."

"What d'you mean – my under arm?"

"It very rude to show your hairy armpit to people in the public!"

In the blink of an eye Natalie's expression turned from one of supreme happiness to one of complete devastation. She glared thunderously at Vince before stomping back towards the gateway of The Karot.

The storm of fury that embodied Natalie's rapid departure,

which was almost as culturally insensitive as displaying her underarms to the distinguished guests, had a number of results.

Firstly, the wedding guests were left halfway through an unusual karaoke rendition of YMCA, being vocally presented in part by an elderly grandmother, with no-one really knowing what to do about that, dance-wise, beyond the uncomfortable point to which they'd already progressed.

Secondly, and perhaps more significantly, as Natalie stormed off, she inadvertently knocked into one of the fold-up tables under the dining awning, causing it to collapse.

In the same way that a hazard such as a typhoon only becomes a disaster once it impacts on a human population, the hazard of the table collapse was considered very much more disastrous once it was evident that a large plate of uneaten seaprawns were deposited into the lap of the mother of the bride. This was further compounded by the realisation that a bucket full of ice cubes and cold water had been poured squarely into the lap of the district police commissioner.

As the family rushed to aid the distressed mother and her hired frock, and the deputies rushed to fawn with sympathy and tissue paper around their damp superior, the microphone sizzled with more feedback and static.

"Time for another classic, Mr. Vanarith. '*Especially for Yaw.*' – I'm gonna be Kylie!"

The call

Vince rolled over towards the bedside table in response to the duel disturbance of his mobile phone ringing and then vibrating manically as if it was trying to drill down through the laminated plastic and break through to the top draw. Neither interruption was really helping with his karaoke and beer induced headache, which would have appreciated a restful lie-in and not an early morning wake-up. He reached across to his side, knocked a few random objects such as his sunglasses and wallet from the small table onto the floor, and eventually achieved contact with the phone through a process of unenthusiastic trial and error. As he squinted at the aggressive object through his blurry, unfocused eyes he could make out on the screen that it was a call from America. He pressed the small button with the green phone icon on it and held it to his ear.

"Yam alright there, Mr. Fairchild?"

In the same way that, for some time, the default international language has been an oxymoron termed 'US English', Fairchild operated on the assumption that everyone was set to the default 'US Time'. Analogous to the way that his laptop determinedly claimed that there was no 'U' in colour or that centre should end in an 'ER', it also convinced him that the only possible time in this brave new world of technology was the one displayed in the bottom right corner of his computer screen. Therefore, US Time on his computer screen in Ohio said 4.00pm, so 4.00pm it must be. This, however, didn't really take into account the 3.00am aspect of time in the location his communication was being directed.

"Vince, it's Jonathan."

There was a pause. Fairchild was clearly expecting a response to this announcement. However, Vince was never strong on responses, even at his most awake, and so at 3.00am he was not in a sufficiently coherent state to develop something suitably articulate on the spot. Fairchild decided to continue anyway.

"I've been reviewing some things, Vince. Well, really 'we've' been reviewing some things. That is to say, Susan and I."

Fairchild paused again, giving the option for Vince to enter into the dialogue.

Vince continued to remain mute. Clearly the onset of his headache, which coincided with the phone waking him, had momentarily taken over the part of his brain from which spontaneous conversation could be initiated.

"So. Reviewing. Anyway, we've been thinking, Susan and I, that the whole hotel thing in Asia is a bit of a mistake. It all came up when we were honeymooning out there, and looking back, Susan has helped me to realise that it was all a bit silly. She's made me realise that it was a crazy time in our lives, and I got caught up in the moment. I was all impulsive, not thinking straight. Sometimes people do silly things when they're in love."

Both Fairchild and Vince then collectively sustained a long pause. Fairchild wasn't good at breaking bad news and he was even worse at expressing emotions or talking about personal things. Uttering the word 'love' out loud had put him completely off his flow. Vince's reasons for a lack of further dialogue had been carried over from the previous lack of dialogue.

Eventually Fairchild had another stab at getting to his point.

"So you see, Vince, Susan's helped me see the error in this scheme. Now is not a good time for me to be starting up hotels in a far off continent. I don't have the time. Especially now I have a wife and commitments here in the US, as well as in the UK. No, I'm afraid this has all been a big mistake. I can no longer be a part of this venture."

In the background Vince could hear Susan, the despicable woman that had conned the malleable Fairchild into unnecessary wedlock, shouting at him to finish the call and get ready as they were going out soon.

"Sorry, Vince, must go. Anyway, as I say, whatever has been spent so far on the business set up I'll cover, of course, but from now on I'm afraid you're on your own. Good luck."

"Bye, Mr. Fairchild."

Vince's capacity to respond arrived slightly too late for the conversation. Just as Fairchild had put down the phone at his end, in fact. However, it would have been irrelevant to debate the decision. Clearly, Vince wouldn't be negotiating with the person who made the decisions in that partnership, and Vince had never been very popular with the former Mrs. Susan Ratcliffe.

The call from Fairchild was brief and awkward, and yet the message was clear. Even in Vince's half-asleep state he was able to understand the implications of what had been said. Susan had crossed his path once again and the result was predictably unfavourable.

Vince attempted to replace the phone on the edge of the bedside table. His failure in this was announced by the clattering noise on the floor as the mobile arrived on the ground and separated itself from its back cover, battery and sim card. This audible declaration of apathetic collapse was the last thing Vince knew before falling back to sleep.

Chapter 2 – School

First day

One week later…

Vince cautiously opened the front door of the German-owned English Language Centre and stepped in. He squinted a little as his eyes adjusted from the intense light of the Khoyleng streets to the strip-light supported reception area of the foyer. As he looked around he noted the office manager's door to his right, a hall in front of him leading to some other rooms, and a group of people having a discussion around a table to his left.

An expression of mild confusion spread across his face when he realised that it was his own nan who was sitting at this corner table with a small group of six students. With a bemused expression, Vince approached his aging relative to enquire as to her presence.

"Yaw right there, Nan?"

"Vince! Alright? I'm just teaching some English grammar to these local kids."

Vince nodded. It was just about a plausible explanation. He had, after all, found his nan in an English teaching school building, and she was surrounded by some attentive youths. In most situations that would have been enough to convince someone that this was the truth. However, this was Vince's nan, so it was never wise to leap to a rapid conclusion. As he gazed at the unlikely scene, he noticed there was a set of playing cards in her hand.

"Yaw sure yaw'm teaching them English, Nan? What's with the playing cards?"

"These? It's me travel *Family Fortunes* fun-pack, Vince. I thought it'd be a good way to teach, and useful for them in the future as well. If these kids ever get satellite TV over here then they'll already be able to understand what's going on. And it's in English. Mrs. Barry says Les Dennis is on satellite most afternoons now with *Family Fortunes* repeats. How she can be sat around watching TV in the afternoon, given the state of her kitchen, is beyond me. There were mouse droppin's by the skirting boards next to the tumble dryer last time I was round."

Vince nodded thoughtfully. Not only was he now reasonably convinced that his nan genuinely gave English classes, but he thought it was quite a good idea, using a word game to help move the lesson along, and decided he'd watch a while. After all, at school he'd never learned anything by being taught stuff in the classroom. Normally he'd be staring out of the window counting the minutes until he could get home and watch TV or play on his bike. Any teaching that was less like teaching and more like watching TV or bike riding had to be a good thing.

"Now then kids..."

Vince's nan elaborately drew the first card from the pack.

"Les asked one hundred people: Name a female character from *Coronation Street*. What d'yaw think was the top answer, Sophak?"

Sophak, a young Feiquon lad of about sixteen, just looked blankly back at her.

"Well, I'm not surprised yaw didn't get that, as you've not got satellite yet, now have you? The top answer was 'Hilda' – goin' back a bit, but you could also have had 'Bet', or 'Mavis'. I 'spect Les would do his impression now, if this was on satellite."

"I'll leave you to it then, Nan."

His nan nodded dismissively, engrossed in her lesson:

"Now then kids, Les asked one hundred people: Name one of the wives of Henry the VIII. It's a tough one this. The top answer is an 'Anne Boleyn' apparently – think we'll try a different one. Here we go: Les asked one hundred people: Name a type of shoe. What d'yaw reckon Chamroun? Type-a shoe?"

Vince reached the other side of the room and knocked on the door below the sign marked 'Manager'.

A young woman from within encouraged him to enter.

Teaching

Vince was already 'teaching' his second class of the day when Maly, the office manager who had hired him, came in to check how he was doing. With Fairchild's withdrawal from the guesthouse venture, Vince was no longer financially assured, and needed to supplement his meagre rooftop bar profits, whilst diversifying his portfolio to spread out the financial risk. Teaching a bit of English seemed like an easy way to quickly raise some cash.

"Mr. Vince, how is your class today?"

"Very good, Ms. Maly."

Vince bent down to pick up the two books he'd knocked on the floor as he'd stood up to greet his supervisor, and replaced them on his desk. Two of the girls at the front giggled annoyingly.

"Very good indeed. We were just talking about the different types of money in England, pounds and pence, and how we do a lot of shopping with credit cards these days."

Vince held out some British coins and notes, and Maly nodded with approval.

"Maybe, Mr. Vince, you can discuss in a way which helps the class practise how they would buy things in English?"

"We were just thinking about that, Ms. Maly. After this class we thought we would walk round to the market and do some practise there. Perhaps you'd like to join us?"

Once again Maly responded positively, with an engaging smile. She was becoming impressed with Vince. It was unusual to get someone to teach at the school who had this kind of genuine enthusiasm. Most of the expats that passed through the school were there for the $10 per hour cash to supplement their nightly drinking budget. Vince seemed different somehow.

"I think I would like to come with your class to the market, Vince. Come to the office after class to tell me when you are leaving."

Maly left, and so Vince returned to his room of annoying gigglers.

Vince had never thought of himself as a 'teacher'. In fact, at the age of sixteen he'd been determined never to enter a school ever again. However, at the age of sixteen-and-a-bit he'd then realised he didn't have a back-up plan to 'not going to school', and joined the sixth form so that he could waste two more years failing some A-levels before finally facing the reality that he had to try and join the bottom rung of the workforce.

Teachers were loathsome, sanctimonious creatures never to be trusted, and certainly not something to aspire to. However, at 'Die Englisch Sprechen-Schule' it was very easy to become one, and as a result he'd experienced a sudden U-turn in his attitude. Especially as the school required no qualifications, or prior experience, or teaching skills from their prospective educators (although in terms of its name it did require a sense of irony). The sole requirement was to be a native speaker of the language. Vince's passport at least demonstrated he was officially in that category. Fortunately the students weren't solely reliant on the likes of Vince to deliver their in-depth education. They had a number of proper, well-organised classes with real Feiquon teachers to give them a good grounding in English language skills and theory. The school then invited expats to come and talk with the students in one-hour sessions, so that the students could get used to hearing and understanding foreigners. If they could actually teach them something, then all the better. This was the theory of Maly's boss anyway, who was a foreigner himself.

Maly was far less keen on the process. The expat discussion scheme seemed to attract a lot of short-term tourists and backpackers who were just travelling through, and wanted to get some extra beer money before the next step of their journey. This recruitment strategy didn't marry-up particularly well with the early morning starts that the school required from their teachers to take advantage of the students' availability, before the young employees started their day jobs. Maly suspected the students learned more about how foreigners acted when they were painfully hungover, or what expats looked and smelled like if they'd been up all night partying, and then went straight from the night club to their day job without showering.

Frank Schneider was the owner of 'Die Englisch Sprechen Schule'. He had invested in a number of small businesses in Khoyleng as well as in the coastal town of Dhokratt. These were mainly higher-end hotels and guesthouses which needed

Englisch sprachen-zing staff to cater for the foreign clientele. Such was his need for competent anglophile Feiquons that he decided he would actually set up his own language school. It would work out cheaper than paying for his staff to get endless lessons from other schools, and he'd make a bit of money as well if he was lucky.

Maly, at that time, had been a co-manager at Frank Schneider's main hotel in Dhokratt. However, Frank's ill-tempered wife didn't like her very much, and every day she would find something new about Maly that annoyed her and then immediately go to Frank and complain about her. She would tell him that Maly had been impolite to a customer, or that the guests weren't happy with the room and Maly was to blame. Perhaps the pool area was untidy and so it was Maly's fault. In reality, Frank knew the key problem was that his wife was a sizable German with an insatiable penchant for her native pork-based cuisine. Maly, meanwhile, was of a typically slender and enviable Feiquon figure. An attribute which meant any size-zero ensemble, however cheap and poorly made, draped elegantly on her frame like it was still on the clothes hanger of a fashion designer. This was in contrast to the common challenge for foreigners of looking like they'd been shoe-horned into a sleeping-bag stuff-sack. She was, however, a trustworthy and hardworking employee. She was also polite, chatty, and Frank enjoyed working with her. When the Englisch Sprechen School started, Frank decided it was easier to send Maly to Khoyleng to oversee the day-to-day running of the new establishment. It would be more pleasant to move to a part-time relaxed working relationship, than for both of them to suffer the diurnal envy-soaked erratic rantings of his bratwurst-filled wife.

Wendelin

Wendelin had not always been such a large woman, or cut such an imposing figure. In her youth she had been considered attractive, in a chiselled kind of way. Should the mood lighting be suitably dimmed, some might even go so far as to use words such as slight, delicate, and even dainty for her shoe size. Frank Schneider, wearing his mood-lit beer goggles, had no complaints back in the day, and he paraded her at bars and clubs in front of his mates with the view that she was a trophy to be displayed rather than an embarrassment to be kept from sight. However, since they had moved to Asia, all of that had changed.

In a land where a size zero is actually a medium, and for your average eligible Bavarian, dating a local bachelorette would involve developing a perpetual stoop, it was quite difficult for Wendelin to maintain the constant portrayal of herself as 'slight and attractive arm-drapery'. Meanwhile, many of the expat community with whom Frank hung out had married young local girls who were on a whole different level of 'feather weight' to that of Wendelin's indigenous understanding of boxing divisions. Sadly, the present vision of Wendelin no longer resulted in Frank's ego floating to the top of the pile.

The local competition was not the only challenge to Wendelin's 'arm candy' status. Her creamy white lower legs were the ultimate magnet to flesh-eating flies and skin-piercing irritants. It is said that a mosquito rarely travels more than one hundred metres in its entire lifetime. However, once news of the feast presented by Wendelin's well-hoofed extremities reached the communication hub of the insect grapevines, their usually apathetic attitude towards long distance commuting was immediately transformed by an invigorated desire to cover as much distance as they possibly could. As a result, whilst other slender, young, exotic wives were out in their best frocks, politely shadowing their drunken husbands, Wendelin's outfits would inevitably reflect a need for full length clothing and thick, ungainly socks with moon-boots to match, to avoid looking like the un-dead from the knees downwards.

It seems that if, due to the myriad of red sores, bites and

scabs, an ankle is no longer to be displayed to impress, then the need to focus efforts in the retention of its elegant structure is also considerably reduced. When this perpetual downward spiral of aesthetic aspiration persists then the long term motivation in maintaining that ankle, or indeed the body attached to it, and the elegance of the clothing there on, will inevitably wane as well.

As is the case with many unhappy people, for Wendelin comfort food had become part of her treatment. Her broad shoulders could no longer carry the weight of the social pressure. The resulting dietary needs meant that her fluctuating metabolism was no longer synchronised with the evolving exotic motivations behind her husband's libido.

Maly had been a problem for Wendelin from the moment she arrived at the Schneider's coastal hotel. Maly did not follow instructions. She was not efficient. She did her own thing. If, in frustration, Wendelin re-issued an instruction about hotel management, the little imp would go to Frank to get his permission first. Meanwhile, in Frank's eyes Maly could do no wrong. With her petit figure, deep eyes, long flowing hair and polite, subservient attitude, she was the mirror image of the bland wives of expats that Frank jealously coveted. Maly would flirt with Frank; not enough to lead him on, but just enough to make him putty in her hands. One evening the little dance between Frank and Maly became too much, and Wendelin confronted him. Loudly. And much to Frank's surprise. Indeed, much to the surprise of a number of the guests, who subsequently chose not to use the hotel's restaurant that evening but to seek out the charms of local street food, which until that point they had determinedly avoided in spite of the guidebook's insistence that it was both a must-do experience and a contribution to maintaining local culture.

The following day, Maly was relocated to the language school in the capital. Wendelin was still unimpressed. If Frank's solution to their marital challenges was to move the temptress to one of his businesses in a different town, so that he could enjoy her without his wife being around, then that was fine. But Wendelin could play that game too.

A few months later, Wendelin met a young guy from the Netherlands. He was staying in their hotel. Meanwhile, Frank was in the capital, no doubt seeing to his interests in the language school arena. Her new man was not ankle obsessed, or wafer obsessed, and a new and delightfully comfortable romance blossomed. However, it was difficult to keep the affair under wraps at the hotel. The staff were Frank's staff. Their loyalties were with the man who signed off on their salaries each month. They were also abundant in number and did a lot of standing around with their hands in their pockets and gossiping. To counter this imposition, Wendelin hatched a plan. She would start up a few businesses of her own in the north of the country. The handsome source of her audacious affair also had work that took him north of the capital on occasion. There would be many opportunities for them to meet up and have wonderful times. As an offshoot to that, she would get her own business portfolio and gain some much needed financial independence from Frank. Wendelin started to feel happier, and the girth of her ankle began to reflect this new self-confidence. Well, a bit anyway.

Market

Laeket Market was located to the east of Stihouasti Road. It was also known as the Kyffoa-Rachey Market. Many of the markets in the Feiquon capital had specialisms. All traders worth their specialist salt would congregate on the basis that a strong association between the product and the location would draw in lucrative custom. As a result, the north of Khoyleng had a famous buffalo market, and the Segona Market on the Jatmee road was famous for fresh fruit and ceramic pots. In the case of Laeket Market, river prawns or 'Rachey' were the goods of notoriety, and a large section beyond the front entrance was dedicated to buckets of grey or pink river crustaceans in varying stages of transition from water dweller to hors d-oeuvre. The additional Kyffoa pre-fix had been added in the 1970s when the market became favoured by Kyffoas (the local term for foreigners, but not including foreign people who were from other parts of Asia), most of whom were of Western decent. These days the part of the market not dedicated to the pursuits of prawn aficionados was a maze of thin walkways filled with abundant treasures for the cashed up tourists. There were high-stacked clothes stalls, wood-carved souvenirs, silks and fabrics, DVDs, and Kyffoas looking to get cheap fake goods to take home to their law-abiding countries. The remaining non foreign-prawn section of the market was a little more conventional, to meet the needs of the local non-Kyffoas, and sold fruit and vegetables, kitchen utensils and other plastic goods, fresh meat, and live fish that sloshed around in buckets on the floor to ensure that customers knew they were getting them fresh.

Vince had decided to start his lecture on 'shopping in English' in the fruit and vegetable section. He already knew how to find a few of the stalls, having done a bit of food shopping there himself.

Vince gathered his students around a vegetable stall where he held up a large cabbage.

"Right then. Who can tell me what this is?"

Before his class could focus on the question, the cabbage

had already been removed from Vince's hand by the nimble and enthusiastic stall owner and quickly became a secure done-deal in a plastic bag at the front of the display. The owner, an elderly but very wise-looking woman, was pointing to the vegetables and talking rapidly to Vince in Feiquon to see what else he could be convinced into purchasing. It was not a good start to his lesson. In fact, Vince felt that the stall owner's post-cabbage-bagging persistence to interest him in a box of sweet potatoes was becoming somewhat of a distraction for the class.

"Maly, perhaps you can explain to the owner of this stall what we're trying to do here?"

Maly quickly spoke to the woman, who nodded sagely to show understanding.

"Now, carrots?"

Vince held aloft a large carrot.

"How would you ask the price of carrots in English?"

"Two-dollar kilo!"

"What?" Vince turned to confront the wizened visage of the stall owner, who had once again disarmed him of his demonstration vegetable, and was putting it in a plastic bag next to the bagged cabbage.

"Two-dollar kilo!" she repeated. "How much kilo you want?"

"Choo Wana! Too expensive, Vince."

Maly had suddenly waded in with a burst of emotion that had previously remained hidden beneath her cool, office manager facade. A heated carrot-debate then erupted between Maly and the old lady on the stall. As it gathered steam, the students also tumbled into the evolving fracas. Vince edged back a couple of steps, feeling rather uncomfortable about his involvement in the whole thing, and watched from a safe distance, as did those from neighbouring stalls, who had looked up to see what the fuss was about.

Maly briefly extracted herself from the fray to enthusiastically update Vince in their progress.

"In the market by my house, I will not pay more than one dollar fifty a kilo for carrots like this."

Having confirmed from Vince's vacant nod that he understood just what was as stake here, and was fully on board with the current events, Maly then returned to join the others. She was like a cowboy in a western, picking herself up from the street and dusting herself down before diving back through the swinging saloon doors to re-join a bar-room brawl.

Vince became struck by the notion that he had very much become the student and not the teacher in the carrot-purchasing exercise. However, he was starting to realise that if all food could be bought like this, he should probably actually pay someone else to do his shopping for him. He'd still spend far less money, even after he'd paid for both the service of a middle-man and the food. Better yet, he could try to persuade Maly to do his shopping for free. She seemed to be enjoying herself, after all.

Vince left the market that morning with a large cabbage and four kilograms of carrots, all of which were surplus to his needs, regardless of how reasonably priced they had become. He decided that his next lesson would be one that taught his students how to take part in a lesson in a market without buying all the examples. On the upside, the excursion had provided an out-of-office environment in which to become better acquainted with his co-worker and students. As they had walked back to the school, weighed down with unrequired vegetables, Vince had persuaded Maly to join him for lunch at some stage, on the pretext that an informal chat about preparation of lessons would be most helpful. In helping to create the opportunity to socialise with Maly, four kilograms of completely unnecessary carrots seemed quite a good deal.

Natalie

One and a bit weeks earlier...

The morning after the wedding party, Natalie had arrived at the airport slightly more furious than when she'd stormed away from the neighbour's wedding celebrations. The armpit hair induced fury had hit a plateau and stayed there since the previous evening. However, there had been the addition of three supplemental mosquito bites inflicted overnight, one of them in fact very near to one of her controversial armpits. This extra infliction had caused the fury level to become marginally elevated beyond the original. The airline people had efficiently updated her open ticket for a seat on the next international flight that morning. They had rarely come across a passenger who looked more wild-eyed and capable of extreme violence. In light of this, regardless of procedure, putting her on the next available plane seemed to be the easiest way to get her out of their airport.

Natalie took advantage of the departure lounge bar and the duty free facilities for topping up her blood-alcohol levels during both her initial departure and the three hour transfer stop. On each occasion she took the opportunity of buying a bottle of duty-free vodka, taking it onto the flight and downing it on route. While consumption of duty-free was not strictly allowed by the airline policy, the air stewardesses took a similar attitude to those of the ticket desk staff. The lesser of two evils meant it was better not to interfere. The woman was clearly trying to deal with her emotions without sharing them or inflicting them on anyone else, which was the proper thing to do. Should those passions spill out beyond the internal, then the stewardesses could end up dealing with a hair-pulling cat fight in the middle of the aisle, so it was far better to let her remain sozzled but silent.

With three hours to go before the impending arrival of her flight in London, Natalie's furious energy finally succumbed to the excesses of alcohol. It was well proven that Natalie's consumption of liquor was exponentially related to her short-term memory capacity. It also seemed to link exponentially to her likelihood of collapse in to an emotionally-charged heap. She was therefore a total mess of weepy sentiment and goo when she reached Heathrow, and eventually staggered with considerable effort and difficulty through the arrival gate, dragging behind her the one of her two check-in bags that she'd remembered to look for.

To Natalie's vodka-induced astonishment, leaning on the barriers waiting to greet her was Nigel Salmon, the dentist. She remembered Nigel from when he used to go to the Carrot and Jam Kettle for a beer at the time when her husband, Dennis, had been running the bar. She couldn't work out how or why he would know that she was coming, but that didn't matter now. At least he was here for her, and that was all that counted.

Natalie abandoned her heavy suitcase in the middle of the walkway and launched herself at speed in a flood of tears and dripping mascara in the direction of the unsuspecting dentist. The people at the barrier adjacent to the dentist, who were waiting to meet up with their own arriving relatives and friends, rapidly stepped back, both in shock at the display of unfettered emotion and as an instinctive reaction to the overwhelming ambience of alcohol that formed a permanent haze around the unstable woman. However, none were more taken aback by this rapid turn of events than Nigel.

Nigel Salmon

Nigel Salmon had been obsessed with Natalie for over three years, which is a long time to desperately crave for the unachievable. He was an educated and rational man and so knew that this was not a healthy way carry on with his life from an emotional standpoint. Unfortunately, it seemed that he just couldn't help it, and regularly cursed his Darwinian survival and reproduction instincts for overriding his daily needs for mundane common sense.

Nigel had first met Natalie when she served him a drink from behind the bar at the Carrot and Jam Kettle. He'd gone to the pub on his own as a kind of 'works Christmas outing'. His battle-axe receptionist had long made it clear that the only social interaction she would consider was when she left the office each day at five on the dot and delivered a glare of contempt by way of a parting salutation. As a result, he'd been the sole representative at his dental practice's annual celebration that evening, and had subsequently positioned himself at the bar where Natalie was serving so it would look less obvious that he was there as a party of one.

Natalie was friendly, attractive, with a bubbly personality, had particularly healthy gums, and clearly followed a very sensible dental hygiene routine. He had mistakenly read her positive attitude towards him as something more than her merely being friendly and doing her job, whilst trying to make her husband a bit jealous at the same time. This was something, when serving behind the bar, that Natalie did with a lot of male customers. For the dentist, it was a wonderful contrast to his usual human interaction. All of the women in Nigel's life were nervous people whinging about pain from within their mouths, demonstrating their erratic fear of drills, and communicating their general ambivalence towards the cost of dentistry services. A chance meeting with a woman exhibiting positive vibes in his day-to-day routine was rarely on the cards, and so the contrast of Natalie had overwhelmed his under-stimulated emotions.

Nigel was a medical practitioner and therefore well aware of the irrational nature of his obsession. He re-read a university biology text about Darwin to remind himself that love was merely a genetic survival tactic to ensure reproduction and short-term nurturing of offspring. It didn't help. Secondly, he followed the time honoured and exploitatively shallow chat-show solution of talking through his problems. However, one-way discussions about unrequited love with people whose mouths were filled with drills, pliers and saliva vacuums whilst having teeth extracted proved less than satisfactory, and a bi-product of this was a slight reduction in clientele. His receptionist was a formidable woman. He was usually too scared of her to even ask who the next patient was, hoping they'd eventually become inquisitive or frustrated enough to wander into the dental room on their own. Therefore, a comforting deep and meaningful with this woman was certainly out of the question. Thirdly, he tried using a dating agency to help him meet alternative women as a way to curb his emotions. There were a few first dates, but at each one he could never get past the fact that the date wasn't Natalie. Also, the women being dated were invariably frustrated when the small talk failed to progress beyond his limited anecdotes relating to wisdom tooth extraction and avoidance of gum disease.

After Nigel's solo and yet inspiring Christmas works outing, Nigel had returned to the Carrot and Jam Kettle a few weeks later on New Year's Eve, spurred on by his recently stirred emotions. He could have sworn that Natalie had been flirting with him. However, shortly after that night he'd learned that she and her husband Dennis were trying for a baby and so he'd kept a low profile. Later in the year he'd found out they'd divorced. His delight in this news was short-lived once he found out she'd immediately shacked up with the new pub owner. This devastating blow had been the turning point that brought on his rapid slide into depression. His clients were increasingly aware of his change of mood, and were overjoyed when they realised it meant that he was so depressed he wasn't even going to bother to start telling them why.

Nigel's ever spiralling decline had accelerated further when he learned that his older brother Thomas, who lived in Canada, was sending his thirteen-year-old daughter Charlotte to stay with him in England for a five-week vacation. He had always been jealous of his brother, whom he felt had hit the jackpot early on in life. His brother ran his own advertising agency, from which he made a lot of money. He was happily married to a beautiful woman living in Canada, and they had a daughter that they doted on. In contrast, Nigel was a depressed and lonely bachelor with no prospect of achieving the stable family life which would eventually lead to doting of any sort.

Nigel, even now, was in Heathrow Airport waiting to receive this annoying thirteen-year-old addition to his depressing existence, whom his brother Thomas had foisted upon him for the summer. He leaned on the barrier in the arrivals lounge and stared vaguely into the middle distance before looking back at the arrivals screen. He noted a flashing announcement next to the Toronto flight showing that it had been delayed by four hours. Nigel sighed in a combination of mild annoyance and apathy. That would amount to almost a whole day wasted just picking up the unwanted guest. As he silently cursed his on-going bad luck, his attention was unwillingly drawn to a family that was loudly exiting the arrival doors. Two parents were being circled by two screeching children who were running around wildly out of control, and another smaller one was being carried by the mother and bawling loudly. Nigel mentally sympathised with the agony of the passengers who had just had the pleasure of their company on a long-haul from the states, and wondered about the future behaviour of the unknown youthful quantity he was about to be subjected to.

As an increasingly embittered bachelor, Nigel had a theory that passengers without kids on planes should get rewarded with 'nursing-home points' via levees on the fare of those who did travel with kids. It followed that these long-suffering passengers did not benefit from the on-going pleasures that kids might bring to their lives, such as the joys of parenthood, having family to look after you in your old age, or at least having someone who might visit you occasionally once you had been stuck in a nursing home. Meanwhile, there was a significant period of time for which childless adults could find themselves unwittingly in close quarters with other people's destructive offspring, and trapped in cattle class was one of these seemingly unavoidable situations. This was commonly a period when these previously unacquainted little bundles of joy were far from presenting themselves at their most delightful. Meanwhile, the childless adult had already had their normal routine disturbed by the unsociable flight scheduling, and just wanted to sleep. Therefore, gathering 'nursing-home points' for suffering such proximity, seemed a very practical way to even things up a bit. When the time came, the points could be exchanged for upgrading your standard class nursing home room for a business class one, or paying for someone to come and visit you in your loneliness.

Nigel's current child-related situation seemed to call for something beyond the nursing-home points theory. He wouldn't just have to endure someone else's kid for the period of a long-haul flight; he'd have to entertain her for a whole five weeks. Nigel didn't feel confident around teenage girls. They usually had an attitude, freaked out loudly and irrationally at the very mention of fillings, and were largely unreceptive to the notion of flossing. It was all so unfair. Not only did his brother strike it lucky with the perfect wife and family, but was also dumping the babysitting of Charlotte onto him for five weeks – all of the problems but none of the benefits.

It was as Nigel reviewed his pit of despair, from which the small circle of light at the top was slowly diminishing, when he spotted Natalie hurtling towards him on the other side of the barrier like a greyhound after a flea-bitten rabbit. Nigel started to mentally note that he really had to get under control his current and slightly unethical habit of inhaling the laughing gas at lunchtimes as a means to give him the motivation to make it to the end of his working day. As he considered this as the root cause of the mirage that was forming before him, Natalie collided heavily with him, grappling him into a bear hug that knocked the air out of him. The physical impact of the woman combined with an overwhelming odour of vodka brought Nigel to the slow realisation that he might not be hallucinating after all.

Heathrow Coffee

Nigel Salmon somehow overcame his embarrassment. He had never been part of a 'scene' before, and the bustling arrivals lounge in Heathrow Airport had seemed a bit of an ambitious venue to make his debut. However, he heroically persuaded Natalie to calm down a little, and then sat her in a coffee shop with a large, expensive designer brew to quaff at, and helped her negotiate her way down the long and blurry road of sobering up.

Half an hour later, Natalie was a little less weepy. A number of tasks had been identified for completion and divided up between them before they could focus on resolving the issue of Natalie's destitution. Having agreed upon their immediate responsibilities, they agreed that they would meet back at the same coffee shop after twenty minutes. This would give Nigel time to negotiate with the airport staff to locate Natalie's remaining suitcase so she could pick it up before they left, and also organise extensive medication for her mosquito bites and hangover. Natalie, meanwhile, would take the opportunity to crawl into a cubicle in the nearby ladies' toilets and chuck her guts up, sounding like a water buffalo that recently mistook some large ripe chillies for oddly shaped but temptingly delicious strawberries. When they reunited, further decisions could be made regarding the need for stomach pumps, depending on analysis of fresh information.

Twenty minutes later, they were back in the coffee shop, and the need for a greasy-spoon breakfast had clearly taken precedence over that for gastric tube-related insertions. Nigel had returned with the suitcase located, and instructions on how Natalie could pick it up, as well as a range of treatments from Boots to repair and sooth Natalie's scab-covered exterior, and alcohol-doused interior. Natalie had returned with slightly watery eyes and an uncomfortable furry sensation on the inside of her teeth. She kept this to herself knowing that mentally she wasn't capable of receiving the dental analysis it might evoke.

There were still more than three hours until the delayed Canadian brat was due. Nigel had agreed that once his brother's offspring was secured he would also give Natalie a lift back to the Midlands, which meant they still had quite a bit of time to kill in each other's company. This additional time spent with the dentist enabled Natalie to deliver the sob story of her travels in immense detail, and communicate to Nigel her concerns regarding her current depth of impoverishment. It also gave Nigel the chance to heroically offer to take Natalie in from the street. He had two spare bedrooms, and the house was big. She could stay with him while she got back on her feet, and in the meantime help him with the challenge of looking after the teenage niece.

Natalie was smitten. She'd had enough of men acting like boys, and boys pretending to be men. This was a real man with a profession, his own business and a large house. He was sensitive and kind. Opportunities didn't come along like this every day so she would have to make sure that she didn't mess it up. Her new goal in life was to become Mrs. Nigel Salmon.

Nigel didn't want to jump the gun, but he could see a lot of potential in Natalie, not only as his future partner but also as a dental receptionist. Being greeted on arrival at the dentist by a woman displaying such finely tended incisors would be enough to inspire any reluctant patient to persist with an extensive programme of corrective dental surgery.

The flight from Toronto eventually arrived and Charlotte, the niece, made it through to arrivals with all of her baggage, and without making an embarrassing scene.

Nigel found it slightly difficult to explain to the teenager that during the time her flight was delayed he'd inadvertently picked up a destitute, mosquito bite-ridden, hung-over woman in the arrivals lounge. He only knew her because she'd served him a couple of times in a bar a year or so ago, and now she was going to travel back home and live with him. However, Charlotte's initial scepticism about being shipped off to the UK for her holidays had been based on her preconception of Nigel being an incredibly dull dentist. As a result of the unlikely explanation for Natalie's random presence, she was more than impressed by the current turn of events and decided holidaying in the Midlands could be quite fun after all.

English

Now that Vince had established himself as a part-time English teacher to supplement his rooftop bar income, he realised just how much of his native language he took for granted, and how little he actually understood about how it all worked. This was unfortunate, as having been at Die Englisch Sprechen-Schule for over two weeks he'd genuinely run out of new things to talk to the students about. Frank Schneider's reason for including expats at the school was so that students could practise listening to and interacting with foreigners. However, if, as was the case with Vince, as a foreigner you'd run out of things to say, then it was difficult to maintain a forum where listening and interacting remained the core outcome. Were Vince to continue teaching from this point forward, then he'd need to actually come up with something to teach.

Since leaving school himself, Vince was increasingly aware that the chief purpose of his native education system, of which he'd been a compulsory recipient, was not education. It was primarily designed to ensure that calm and unruly kids alike, who would otherwise be kicked out of the house for the day, were stored collectively in an enclosed and supervised area nearby to prevent them from running riot in locations assigned for the daytime occupation of adults. Any accidental learning spinning off from this process of social containment was very much a side effect, and rarely amounted to anything of value. Indeed, as Vince analysed this reality in relation to his current dilemma, he struggled to identify anything he had been told at school that he had since applied in his efforts to become employable. All he could come up with was the mathematical ability to work out if you'd got the right change at the shops. However, as the standard cost of everything in the UK ended in 99p, then most of the time the change was 1p, so Vince reckoned he could have still worked this out even in the absence of a twelve-year education. Besides, you could use a debit card for most things these days, so understanding your 1p change was becoming something of a dying art anyway.

In terms of language, Vince recalled he had been instructed

that 'adjectives' described stuff, 'nouns' were the names of things, and that he should then sit down and either just make up a story, or write down what he'd done at the weekend before the bell went at twelve o'clock. After which, he and his fellow yarn-weavers would all be booted outside for an hour to stand around in the drizzle, processing limp and unenthusiastic sandwiches, and possibly kick about a football if someone had remembered to bring one. Pitiful excuse though this was for igniting the life-journey inspiration for young people as they embraced their pathway to a world of enlightened possibilities and vibrant opportunities, it certainly didn't help Vince in his current situation, where he was now responsible for students that were genuinely expecting to be taught something of value. Handing them a postcard and telling them to go and invent a narrative about whatever picture was on it would not inspire them to believe they were any closer to a fast-tracking career as an executive, bringing wealth and stability and ensuring the future wellbeing of their children.

As a result, Vince had bought himself a book from the market about learning the English language, and spent his free time during the day trying to gain some confidence in the purpose of adverbs, pronouns, and conjunctives.

Just two days later, Vince was able to reap the benefits of his research. At a post-market field trip English lesson, Vince threw caution to the wind and decided it was time to talk about the difference between 'there' and 'their'; the latter being more possessive than the former. The result was inspiring. It seemed that much as his students over recent weeks had enjoyed learning from Vince about the roots of heavy metal music, pork scratchings and their role in contemporary international cuisine (or 'what a pork scratching is'), and the confusing wonder of the 'spaghetti junction' road system, they were far more receptive to something that contributed to the development of their language skills. Cultural barriers had finally been broken. A grammatical instruction had succeeded where a bag of crunchy pork rind had failed to impress. So much so that Chamroun and Sophak, who had recently joined Vince for an extra class, invited Vince to come out with them for an evening beer. The two of them were both members of his nan's English class which, once the family fortune travel pack had been exhausted, rapidly deteriorated into a daily pre-work poker game. As much as Chamroun and

Sophak were both gaining considerable skills in bluffing and maintaining a formidable poker face, this skill development was of limited value when working in a hotel reception and politely convincing checking-out guests that all of the items on the receipt were definitely things they had to pay for. Subsequently they'd joined Vince's class as well.

The evening beers started off a little bit awkwardly, and centred on the idea of meeting at a street corner, sitting sideways on the seats of their mopeds, not really doing much, and then going to a noodle shop. However, once Chamroun and Sophak worked out that Vince was paying for the night's indulgences, the suggestion of karaoke was never far away.

It was Vince's first venture into the gritty world of the karaoke bar, and it was an eye opener in many ways. Firstly, having been ushered into a room with a TV and karaoke machine, it was remarkable just how many beer girls suddenly appeared and wanted to help out with the singing. It was all a bit sordid for Vince's liking. He was also surprised at how enthusiastic the guys were at singing loudly, out of tune, and out of time, despite the vast amounts of echo from the microphone with which they tried to cover up these shortcomings. More remarkable was that the output, which to Vince sounded like a damaged sea-lion trapped in a large cave with a disappointing drum machine, was still considered very palatable to the ear by the other participants.

Vince sat with his beer, taking in the scene. Whilst trying to edge away from a particularly enthusiastic beer girl, he had his greatest revelation since developing his career in the education sector. He had watched as Chamroun put *Hotel California* on the karaoke to try to impress Vince with a song in English, and then tried to follow the lyrics as they scrolled across the screen. Vince realised it was the first time since his departure from the UK that he had seen anyone in Khoyleng read something for pleasure. Suddenly the dark shadow of a scheme fell across Vince's inner thoughts and he realised that there was a simple way to retain his teaching job without having to know anything further about grammar or how to teach English. The *Eagles* were going to do all the hard work for him.

His new plan of 'karaoke teaching' was such an innovative way to get out of actually teaching, he was surprised his nan hadn't thought of it first.

A return to trading

You don't need golf to ruin a perfectly good walk. In this part of the world people could stuff up walking perfectly well without any extra motivation whatsoever. This was the cynical conclusion that Vince arrived at as he crossed through the thin bands of open park near the riverfront and made his way towards the restaurant where he would meet Maly. He wandered alongside the miniature lawns and manicured flowerbeds to the sound of the tinny and repetitive synthesised beats that accompanied enthusiastic groups of women doing aerobics. However, it wasn't just the noise that impacted on the walking; it was more that nobody actually just walked in a normal way. They walked and shadow-boxed, or jogged without making any real progress forward. Walkers swung their arms in sweeping side-to-side arcs, or alternated between walking facing forwards for five steps and then in reverse for the next five steps.

In Vince's home town, carrying on like this would result in contempt, derision and being completely ostracised. Here, people were able to get on with their enjoyment of these quirky exercises without others raising an eyebrow, or them being judged derisively by their peers. Or perhaps this was just the equivalent of a normal walk in this particular culture. Vince was still relatively new to the place and didn't want to fall into the trap of thinking he'd got everything figured out in the first few weeks. That sort of closed-minded approach would stifle the delights of his on-going discovery of what 'abroad' was all about. Vince decided that he should delight in the pleasure that people were having, rather than become the cynic that his own culture had conditioned him to be. After all, he had a date with an attractive young lady, and so his happy mood should feed off such enthusiasm.

He wandered back to the roadside and was reminded as he dodged a couple of tuk-tuks that the rejection of a usable pavement system for pedestrians was also one of the walking-related quirks in his new environment that was lost on him.

Vince had been reconsidering the trade-up theory quite a lot of late. According to this theory, he had to trade his entire life every three months until he became a success. This meant a change of job, girl, wheels, threads and house until he became the man he needed to be. Since the plan to move to Asia, this approach to bettering himself had been very much left on the back burner. After all, he had been a businessman setting up a chain of new guesthouses for a rich American company. His former pub boss, Natalie from the Carrot and Jam Kettle, had been his girlfriend. They'd had the business, and a nice apartment. Success had supposedly been achieved, and the need to keep trading up his life had no longer been relevant. This said, of late there had been a sudden turn around regarding his fortunate set of circumstances, and he found that he was now buying an unnecessary amount carrots in exchange for the chance of getting $10 an hour by speaking English to Feiquons to subsidise his failing roof-top bar. And Natalie had walked out on him. This was no longer the dream lifestyle he had been envisaging when he proudly declared to the woman on the check-in desk at Heathrow that he had packed the suitcases himself, before then regretting taking unseen responsibility for whatever his nan had decided was essential luggage for a foreign country.

To this end, he had decided that it was probably worth revisiting his trade system once more, to see how it faired under Asian conditions. Trade one in terms of job, house, threads, girl and wheels, would include being a part-time English teacher and barman, with a small apartment beneath his struggling roof-top bar and threads in the form of a casual T-shirt and trouser combination. Acknowledging that two key elements were yet to be established, he could trade his way up the ladder again from there. Having reignited the trade up system, the next priority was to deal with the question of the girl. Maly had shown herself to be pleasant and amiable, whilst having proven talents in vegetable negotiation and procurement based scenarios. She might very well be worth pursuing.

Vince arrived at the restaurant where he had agreed to meet Maly. He sat at an empty table by the road side, ordered a coke and stared out at the busy street whilst he contemplated the hectic changes in his own life of late.

The morning after the street wedding, Vince had woken up on his own in a spare guest room. Obviously he had not had the courage the previous evening to return to Natalie, but had waited until she had calmed down and sobered up a bit. It had been a particularly wise move in light of the phone call he had received in the middle of the night from his benefactor.

Vince had spent most of the morning lying on the bed in the guest room, watching a small lizard as it meandered around the ceiling whilst carefully not giving away any clues for the reasoning behind such purposeful yet random activity. He contemplated how to tell Natalie that Fairchild had pulled the plug on their guesthouse career. He also contemplated how to find some paracetamol on the lower floor of the building without crossing Natalie's path before he'd worked out what to say.

Fairchild's news had been very badly timed. Of course Vince himself was extremely upset by the turn of events. However, in Natalie's heightened state of distress the added information that they were now probably jobless and soon to be cast out onto the streets, was likely to be more than she could take without having a total breakdown. When Natalie's husband had left her the previous year she had taken to moping around in batik jangly clothes for several months. Vince assumed at the very least that her reaction would see her draped from head to foot in local scarfs and weavings, and then signing herself up to several traditional cultural dance classes by the end of the week. However, there were a number of worst case scenarios that had also crossed his mind, which even made flouncing about to poorly tuned bamboo xylophone music seem the lesser evil.

By the time the fug of Vince's head had cleared enough to try to communicate with Natalie, he found that the apartment beneath the roof top bar was absent of any trace of her. She, her clothes, and her suitcase were all gone, along with passport, return ticket, and money. On the bedside was a large can of mosquito spray with a note taped to it which read: *At least I won't be needing this anymore!*

Vince was very upset, but also a little relieved. They had been good together at the Carrot and Jam Kettle. It had all made sense. In Feiquon, Natalie had been more than a fish out of water; she had been like a pork chop in a vegetarian restaurant. Things had made far less sense. Her reluctance to participate and her determination to avoid the bright side, combined with a severe mosquito paranoia, had rather beaten the fun out of the relationship. Having avoided a confrontation about the wedding debacle, a confrontation about the Fairchild debacle, and a debacle over what they would have to do next to avoid a further debacle, Vince was actually quite glad that Natalie had walked out on him.

Once the gossip of Natalie's impassioned departure was out in the open, Mr. Piseth the landlord had asked Vince to stay on at the guesthouse and help to run the bar. Obviously Piseth was very grateful that Vince had turned up out of the blue a few months earlier, and financially supported him to finish the construction of his ill-financed building and turn it into a guesthouse. However, Mr. Piseth did not have the knowledge, experience or the inclination to run a rooftop bar. Therefore, it was agreed with Vince that if Mr. Piseth got to keep the furnishings for the rooms, then he and his family would run the guesthouse. Meanwhile, Vince could stay in the apartment and have free reign to manage the bar. Mr. Piseth knew nothing about running a bar, but did know enough to see that it made the guesthouse seem a more attractive and convenient option, and so for him it was a win-win situation. Vince retained Sophea in his employment, providing her with a lateral career transition from concierge to publican, and taught her the basics in the art of enabling people to get drunk.

Lunch

There were two main advantages of travelling in a part of the world that was once colonized by the French. The first was that their passion for food clung to their old abode like the early morning dew on a fresh blade of grass, and emanated into the very lifeblood of the culture. Arguably then, their greatest legacy to the benefit of the modern traveller, despite the passing of the years and the changing social and economic landscape, was that fresh bread was nearly always available in some form or other, regardless of the political 'ism' of the day. Secondly, and almost as importantly, the French left behind the metric system.

The modern definition of the metre is, of course, the length of the path travelled by light in vacuum during a time interval of 1/299,792,458 of a second. At the time of colonisation, it was defined by a metal stick kept in the International Bureau of Weights and Measures in Sevres, France. Its dimensions were based on a fraction of a meridian arc, calculated by working out the distance between the Dunkerque Belfry and Montjuic Castle in Barcelona, and then presumably doing some very complicated long division. It is therefore thanks to eminent Frenchmen studying distances between belfries and castle towers, with the subsequent crafting of sticks, that maths has remained so sensible in a number of exotic lands ever since.

In contrast, travelling to a country formally considered to be a British territory may well provide the opportunity to communicate a need for bread without having to invest time in mastering complex linguistic skills to do so. However, it is far less likely that any bread is actually going to be available once this request has been put forward, and therefore will not be produced in response to that communication. As a result, not only are travellers limited to ordering whatever food is locally available, for which they may have to learn a new word anyway, but the chances are, that depending on the form that this nutrition takes, it is very probable that it needs to be ordered by the square foot.

Maly arrived at the restaurant and, following some initial

pleasantries, they perused the glossy menu. The various European historical to-ings and fro-ings over the past centuries that had preceded Vince's arrival meant that he could employ his 'eating on a first date' theory, and he immediately ordered a ham sandwich with soft white bread.

Vince's theory of 'eating on a first date' was a simple one, following the hypothesis that in the event that you've somehow scored a one-off chance to impress a delicate beauty of the opposite number, the most likely outcome is that you're going to inadvertently make an idiot of yourself within the first five minutes. Therefore, pre-empting this idiocy, and identifying all the obstacles that might otherwise prevent you from retaining any sense of dignity by the end was just common sense.

The first logical step involved ordering food that did not make you seem utterly incompetent in the most basic skill of feeding yourself. To manage such eating challenges, there were certain food categories identified in the theory of 'eating on a first date' to be avoided. This extended to dribbly food, for example noodles with chopsticks, where you would encounter an inevitable and relentless clump of knotted pasta that couldn't be vacuumed towards your jowl in one attempt. The part still hanging from your mouth would require further shovelling, using utensils that were ill-designed for the task and for which you had limited skills anyway. Alternatively, if the crunching of your food being reduced by your molars meant that your date had to raise her voice to the point that the other diners were more focused on her dialogue than their own meals, then your choice of food hadn't done you any favours. Similarly an ambiance of you 'chewing the cud' would present your date with a sense of having wandered into a field of Friesians rather than the opportunity to engage with the man of her dreams.

Breadsticks and other crumby substances could result in you becoming obsessively preoccupied in constantly brushing way the result of your grazing from the front of your shirt, rather than enquiring the opinion of your date with insightful questions then feigning unabated interest at the answers. Stringy food should also be avoided at all costs. Scientists had spent decades trying to perfect a marketable substance to imitate the feet of geckos as they effortlessly glue themselves to the ceiling. However, it seemed to Vince that a stringy bit of chicken and the teeth at the front of your mouth held all the answers.

A final consideration, for those feeling really confident in their flirtation skills, was to avoid anything that you thought might make you break wind repeatedly in the following twelve hour period.

It was remarkable to Vince that the male of the species had not yet figured out a way to remove 'eating together' from the socially expected arsenal of initial ways to impress. As a courting methodology it invariably increased the risks of physical embarrassment, whilst having limited impact on taking a relationship to a higher level. It did, however, provide an uncomfortable space in which to listen and observe someone else process and digest food. It also had the potential to create endless conversational vacuums in which to verbally trip yourself up as you stared at each other across a small table in a quiet restaurant, wishing the starters would arrive to give one of you something to say. However, in these post- 'meat-and-two-veg' days of modernity, eating seemed to be an even more popular option for creating a bad first impression than ever before.

Philosophy

Vince had certainly not been expecting that the lunch conversation between himself and Maly would be dominated by discussions about beliefs. Particularly those beliefs he thought he'd left well behind him when he'd ascended from the Heathrow tarmac to the soundtrack of his nan chewing loudly on three pieces of gum. This, she had assumed, would stop her eardrums from bursting as the aeroplane took off, but it merely had the effect of gluing her dentures together.

Maly, it seemed, was a member of a church group that held services in town every Sunday. They had social events during the week and did good deeds for poor villagers in remote parts of the country. To Vince, it was all very impressive. He had never really followed religion. Other than an occasional hymn in assembly at school, most of his limited knowledge came from an *AC/DC* song. Having initiated creation and conveniently come up with the idea of guitars and drums very early on in the process, by around about the fifth day the deity had declared, 'Let there be Rock'. From this point forward, the post-creation period that followed was satisfyingly all about loud bluesy riffs and rock 'n' roll.

Vince dragged himself away from memories of a concert he'd gone to at the NEC with his cousin Justin on the *Ballbreaker* tour, and tried to listen to Maly instead.

"We are building a new church in a village. It is in one of the provinces a long way from the capital. We have given them clean water and clothes, and built a new roof for their classroom and given them books. The pastor and some of his people help local children and even adults in the district to learn to read. The schools are not very good in that area. In some villages there are rural people who don't speak the same language as us. We help them to learn to read by teaching them some simple prayers. I was invited to visit the village last year. All the people were very happy that the church had sent us there to be with them."

Vince's ability to vocalise an opinion about supernatural belief systems was similar to his capacity to explain to an air stewardess why he was presenting her with a set of cemented teeth belonging to the elderly passenger next to him, and what outcome he was hoping for should the stewardess agree to take temporary possession of them. He decided to focus on the more practical elements of the story.

As Vince struggled to think about churches, his mind was cast back to run-down churches in the Midlands where the signboards outside the gates requesting money to patch up leaking roofs had been there so long they needed money to be renovated themselves. It was not a symbol of an institution with prosperity and a high income.

"How did a church find the money for that sort of thing?"

"We have some pastors that come from America. They help us to find money from other members of the church in America. They gather lots of money from people who want to help us. We are very lucky. Some of the church members are now studying to become pastors as well, so they can help others in the country to learn more."

"But don't you already have a religion, Maly? I thought you were all Buddhists, what with the temples and all the orange monks wandering about? Why is it better to swap to a new faith rather than be a Buddhist? Especially when you already are one."

"The pastors, they explain this very well, Vince. The Buddha was a man from India many centuries ago. He sat beneath the Bodhi tree and learned four noble truths about suffering. Buddha wants us not to suffer, so we should stop to desire permanent things, to be unselfish, and to break the cycle of death and rebirth. Buddhists can be good people, but they are still atheists and need guidance. They pray to the Buddha, but he was a man, not the creator. It is important that we understand the difference so that we can go to heaven."

Whilst Vince tried to take onboard the contradiction of Maly's delightful traditional Feiquon demeanour and yet the evident out-right rejection of her ancestors' culture, she leaned forward and asked him a question:

"If you were to die today and you are facing your creator when he asked you 'Why would I let you into this Heaven?' what would you answer to him?"

Vince thought for a while before answering. "I don't know, Maly."

"I'd probably try and find out what answer he'd given when

it was his go. It must have been all right if he then got the job of asking all of the others."

The need to demonstrate how quickly he could think on his feet in the event that, whilst dealing with the emotional trauma of losing his life and passing from his physical world, a deity would hit him with a one-chance quick-fire question to make it into eternity all seemed a bit suspicious. Vince felt like he was talking directly to one of the pastors who was channelling through Maly, rather than actually having a conversation with Maly anymore. Perhaps that was how these belief systems worked. Vince decided to throw a tangent into the conversation. Spiritual beliefs and politics are as unlikely to support the successful outcome of a first date as ordering something that is dribbly, crunchy, crumby, hot, mobile, stringy or chewy from the menu. Instead, Vince decided to tell Maly all about a trail bike tour he was thinking of going on.

Chapter 3 – Bikes

Karot locals

The clientele at The Karot Rooftop Bar had not evolved as Vince would have predicted. (It should be noted that post-Natalie, Vince had dropped the 'Lu Goccelu Yak' thing as he could never remember it, and it was very confusing to the Feiquon staff and customers as well. In fact, the landlord had taken down the sign over the guesthouse and replaced it with something in Feiquon script which, when explained by Sophea, seemed equally unpronounceable. Vince understood that it included the word 'lucky' to make sure that it would be, but despite this, he had decided it wasn't worth the effort to try and remember that either. Instead he'd got Sophea to get an extra sign made for 'The Karot Rooftop Bar' with a picture of a carrot and a glass of beer on it, and hung it next to the landlord's new sign.)

Vince had been expecting to attract a few local Feiquons who might find it a convenient place to escape their nagging wives for an early evening drink before moving onto the karaoke bars, and for a few tourists to pepper the array of comfortable seating that overlooked this lofty segment of breezy suburbia. In fact, The Karot's most regular customers to prop up the bar were two blokes who ran trail bike tours, his nan, and Mr. Vanarith the document man.

The trail bike duo ran their business from a house at the end of the street. They were both in their late thirties or early forties, a bit older than Vince. 'Choc' was a British expat who seemed to be very self-assured and confident. He was friendly enough, but came across as the type of person who always had an angle on things and you could never be quite sure whether to trust them. 'Lamb', meanwhile, was his side kick. He was a tall Dutchman who towered over Vince, almost as though he was there as Choc's bodyguard.

Choc and Lamb were delighted when The Karot became a feature of their chosen residential street. Whilst the area had a number of draws, not least of all the low rent, the lack of a decent bar within walking distance had always been a distinct disappointment. Secondly, Choc and Lamb ran trail bike tours for locals and tourists alike, which would leave from their ground floor garage very early in the morning and often return late in the evening a few days afterwards. The frustrations of clients not turning up on time in the morning, or whinging about being back too late after the trip could both be addressed by teaming up with the recently renamed 'Lucky Lucky Goose-Dragon Lucky Guesthouse' to provide reasonably priced accommodation for both pre and post departure. This was explained at length to Mr. Piseth the landlord, who was keen to secure their regular trade, and he even offered a five per cent discount for them. It had been on the evening that Choc and Lamb propped up the bar following the securing of this financial bargain, that Vince had become enthralled with the idea of trail biking.

"Yaw seem to have a great job there, Choc, riding motorbikes for a living. How easy is it to ride one of them trail bikes? I've seen them on the TV when they'm racing in the mud. Is it a bit like that, or more like getting where you're going on a bicycle, but not having to do the pedalling?"

"You've got to be quite fit to ride one of these bikes like we do, Vince. It takes strength to handle the bike properly once you're out of the city and on the dirt roads. Isn't that right, Lamb?"

"Yeah, it's right."

"Yaw grand-dad used to take us all over the pissin' countryside on his motorbike with me in that pissin' sidecar of his, Vince."

"Sounds like you guys really know your stuff. I wouldn't mind having a go myself. Maybe on one of the shorter trips you do, where they stay overnight in a village and then come back the next day. Just to get a feel for it, like."

"You might be in luck Vince. We've got a two-day trip going on Monday to Laekhoe Province, isn't that right, Lamb?"

"Yeah, it's right."

"You could leave the girl of yours in charge of the bar for a couple of days and come along."

"'Course, it was all dirt roads and small lanes back then, and me with me pissin' piles bouncing around on my arse in that tin can on the side. Not that your grand-dad ever cared, mind."

"I guess I'd have to buy a trail bike to be able to go along then, Choc. Is it expensive to get one round here?"

"We've got bikes you can hire. Lamb and I work on them during the day to make sure they're serviced properly. It's all part of the tour package. We can give you a bit if a discount if you like. In return it'd be good for our business if we could put a few fliers on your bar, and then if you've been on one of the tours you'll be able to tell people what to expect."

"To be quite honest with you, I was quite relieved when he finally died and I could start taking the pissin' bus again."

Mr. Vanarith's interest peaked at this point. He'd never quite worked out Vince's nan's marital status, and was concerned that there might be a husband around from which she wasn't entirely separated. Divorces could be socially difficult for families, so a low-key separation was often opted for in the name of dignity. However, whilst this addressed the immediate family concerns regarding embarrassment, it could be far less helpful for the separated couple to move on with their lives. The low-key dignity thing could also make it difficult for the potential future wooer to work out the situation of the separated as well.

"Yaw make it all sound fantastic, Choc. I'm definitely up for it, but I'll need to learn to ride the motorbike first. You know, have a bit of a practice."

"Your grand-dad tried to teach me to ride his pissin' motorbike once. Sat me on it, and kick-started it. Told me to just open the throttle and kick the pissin' thing into gear."

"You can come over tomorrow, Vince, and we'll get you organised. Maybe you can wander over around ten, and we'll find a bike for you to try."

"By the end of the street, I was lying in the gutter, and the bike was halfway through the butcher's front window. We were pulling white-washed splinters and pieces of glass out of the mince for weeks afterwards, once we'd paid for the damage and had to buy all the pissin' meat that had been in the front of the shop."

Mr. Vanarith held Vince's nan's hand in a comforting way and asked Sophea to pour her a gin and tonic. It sounded like all the biker discussions with Choc had stirred up some very painful memories.

Charles Cadby

The naming of an English child is a very serious thing. Expectant parents will spend months agonising over what name to give their miracle unborn offspring. Fortunately, there is a whole industry of baby-name books and websites to help with this. Family meetings will often lead to a former or dying relative's name being wedged into the shortlist, resulting in large fallings-out within families should the wedging prove to have been unsuccessful. Meanwhile, the future parents will spend days and days going through all of the people they've been exposed to throughout their schooling and adult life to make sure the final name choice for junior doesn't remind either one of them of a person that they previously detested or even found mildly abhorrent. Having eventually agreed on the preferred moniker that this new life should carry throughout their forthcoming existence, once produced, the new infant and its name will be registered formerly with the government. Many families will even go to the extent of religious ceremonies to further ingrain the inseparability of name and being.

Logically, it should then be of great surprise to us, that within a few years of this long and drawn out process, many people will not be using their given name at all as a way of identifying themselves in social circles. If lucky, then a shortened version of their name will be used. However, it might then get lengthened again with a 'y' (e.g. Nicholas to Nick to Nicky), and if the first name isn't suitable for this process then it will be dropped altogether, and the surname will be modified and used for identification in a similar way. All of this effort, it seems, is to enable the public to avoid using the perfectly socially acceptable name that people started out with in the first place. In some cases, a short name will be used that is supposed to officially represent that actual name, but is not, in fact, in the least bit similar, like 'Bill' instead of William. In the worst case scenario, a person will have acquired a nickname not based on their original name at all. For example, someone caught in an experimental situation with a basket of vegetables might earn themselves the name 'Asparagus', or 'Tuber'. Despite the brevity and 'one time-ness' of the unfortunate act that earned them this, it will no doubt haunt them for the rest of forever, unlike their actual name, which, in contrast, their parents may have spent months and months agonising over.

It is even more surprising then, that we are not all surprised by this, given the immense effort and numbers involved when trying to come up with a suitable name in the first place.

Charles Cadby was no exception to the widespread inability of the population to respect the name that people are given at the event of their birth. A slightly rotund kid, his form added to the perfect storm that swirled around him. His first name had already been shortened by his parents, as fans of Mr. Berry the Rock and Roll singer, to 'Chuck'. His surname was very similar to that of a famous chocolate factory, and so the inevitable and yet obvious deviation was never far away. By the age of seven, even his parents only ever called him 'Choc'. Life can be cruel that way.

Choc's school life was relatively uninspiring, as you would imagine for a kid who was slightly chubby and referred to by both students and teachers alike as 'Choc-y'. Whilst a magnet for bullies, and consequently repellent to girls, Choc managed to stand up for himself most of the time, but inevitably became fairly bitter about his lot in life. This bitterness could have eaten away at him throughout his life, had it not been for him arriving in an exotic Asian land during a spot of post-university travelling.

Feiquon was the childhood that Choc never had. In the preceding years he had gained a bit of height, started going to a gym and had lost his extra weight. He was therefore well placed to step into a new environment without his physique being anything but a good thing, and with the option to go by whatever name he chose. Not only was he getting a fresh beginning in a new place, but despite the fact that he continued to habitually refer to himself as Choc, the story behind his name was never questioned by anyone, nor did anyone care. Secondly, and perhaps more importantly, Feiquon was the perfect place for grown men from the West to become adolescent children again, and get away with it.

At the heart of this phenomenon was the fact that there were very few rules, and there were almost no rules that could not be broken without a wad of dollars being able to make the problem go away. Things that Choc would never do in England suddenly became a right in Feiquon. Following road rules or wearing a motorbike helmet would not only be things Choc would do without question in his home country, but he would even voice strong conservative opinions about those who failed to respect the laws of society. In Feiquon, ripping round the streets on a big bike, with no helmet, jumping the lights on an unregistered vehicle and having no driving licence, the same as everyone else, was just part of the culture. Similarly, going to seedy bars and picking up rough-looking prostitutes in the UK was something that Choc thought that rough seedy-looking people did. It was not something Choc's pride would let him stoop to. However, in contrast, Choc was fine with going to expat bars in Feiquon until late in the evening, flirting with the beautiful Feiquon girls, buying them drinks all night and paying them to go home with him. In Feiquon, this type of seediness was a quite different thing, very common amongst people just like him, and perfectly acceptable within the confines of his morality. If Choc wanted to set up a business in Feiquon, then he could just do it. He'd find a local silent partner, or just pay some cash to the right people, and off he went. There were no tax returns to fill, compulsory insurance, employee rights and pensions to pay or have a moral dilemma over. If you knew how to make a bit of money then you could go ahead and do it, and all wrapped within the warm, snug sunshine of a tropical country.

The lifestyle and environment suited Choc just fine, and he decided to stay.

Learning to ride

At 9.50am Vince was waiting outside the door of Choc's residence and ringing the bell. Vince had never ridden a motorbike before. In the last few months he'd been on the back of the small mopeds that were used as slightly wobbly taxis to ferry people around the city. He'd never been in charge of one though. Also, the high-riding trail bikes that Choc and Lamb used were far bigger and more intimidating than the street motos. His new trade-up was in full swing, he had the bar, the teaching, a T-shirt with a local beer written on it, and had been on a lunch date with Maly. The big gap that currently gaped in his trade-up portfolio was the wheels. He'd briefly considered getting a moto. However, the 'trade-up' was all about ambition and the moto didn't really seem to fit. No – big off road trial bikes that made grown men look like superheroes but enabled them to act like children at the same time were the only way to go. In a culture where macho gestures were what counted, and nothing smaller than a black 4x4 twice the width of most roads, fitted with tinted windows, was good enough to send your wife to the shops in, a 120cc moto was never going to give him the edge with Maly. He'd check out the trail bike scene on this first trip, and then look into buying his own bike after that.

Vince had heard that there was a certain age people reached, beyond which if you'd never bungee jumped or sky-dived then you probably never would. Your idiot-gene would have degenerated sufficiently so that your sense of self-preservation protected you from such things. Vince began to worry that he might face the same problem with the trail bike, so it was better to get on one as soon as possible. He was fairly confident that even in the worst case scenario he was unlikely to send the machine on its own through a glass-fronted shop window. The absence of an unwieldy side-car welded to the frame of any of Choc and Lamb's bikes, as well as the absence of any glass fronted shops on their particular residential street meant that the odds were very much with him in this particular case.

Lamb wandered out of the front gate looking bleary-eyed

and tall. He pulled the left half of the gate to the side and motioned for Vince to come in.

"I'll fetch Choc."

Vince nodded and watched the sarong-clad, muscle-toned, verbally-economical Dutchman wander back inside the building. Lamb wasn't much for conversation and Vince couldn't remember a time when he'd said more than three words in one go. He assumed that would probably all change once they were biker-mates, sharing tales of off-road adventures. The garage was opened and Vince squeezed his way past an old hardtop Land Cruiser on his way to the back of the room to check out the bikes. There were seven lined up at the side of the garage, and then two really big ones parked in a less regimented line next to the Land Cruiser. Vince assumed that these were Choc and Lamb's trusted steeds. They were certainly very large and impressive. Vince decided to study the smaller ones to see which of them looked more suitable as a training bike for him.

"Mornin' Vince."

Vince turned round to see Choc standing in the entrance of the garage with his hands on his hips.

"Yaw've got some great looking bikes in here, Choc."

"I reckon we'll start you off on the Honda XLR, Vince. That one in the corner. Do you want to wheel it out to the street? I'll get my bike out the way for you. Try not to scratch the Land Cruiser while you're at it."

Vince started to push the bike from off its stand and tried to move it forward. He was amazed how heavy it was. He'd assumed the whole point of these plastic-looking trail bikes was that they'd be light so they didn't get stuck, and were easy to pick up if you came off in the mud. He also hadn't got used to the way that motorbikes were all named with a string of random letters. Cars had names like Sierra, Cooper, or Polonez, so it was easy to distinguish between them. Not only did motorbikes fail to benefit from this practical system, but also Choc and Lamb seemed to delight in reciting these letter-names as if they were a secret code to their biking conversations, so that others would just have to be impressed rather than understand.

Vince eventually negotiated his way onto the street and carefully put the bike back on its stand next to Choc's. The advantage of living on a fairly quiet side street was that learning to ride a bike should be possible without an audience of intrigued locals and their children waiting to see if you'd fall off so they could laugh at you. The disadvantage for Vince was the discovery that his nan had felt obliged to take on this role in their absence, and had rounded up Mr. Vanarith, Mr. Piseth, Sophea and some of the guesthouse staff to help. All of them were currently lined up on the side of the street under the shade of a wall waiting expectantly to be entertained.

"Get on the pissin' bike then Vince. We've not got all day."

It did seem to be a quirk of the British to voluntarily turn up for something for which they had not been specifically invited or paid (school yard fights, jumble sales, that sort of thing), and then get frustrated if it didn't then fit with the window of time they'd allocated to it.

Despite his nan's heckling, Vince climbed on to the bike. He was relieved to note that the ride height had reduced considerably as a result of his weight pushing down on the shock absorbers. He looked to Choc for some guidance. Choc then talked him through the starter, gears, clutch, and brakes. In contrast to Vince, Choc quite enjoyed getting to show off to his audience. Being seen to be cool and knowledgeable around big bikes was all part of the expat childhood that Choc delighted in.

Eventually, following a pre-cursor of a couple of false starts and stalls, Vince made a shaky run to the end of the street. By the time he returned to Choc's house he was beginning to remember that the lever by his left hand was a clutch and not a brake, and by the time he'd gone round the block two minutes later he considered himself to be a pro. He might even consider going to buy a motorbike helmet later in the day if he could find one that both looked cool and wouldn't feel too uncomfortable in the tropical heat. Most importantly, Vince had gained the self-belief that he was now an indestructible biker just the same as Choc and Lamb. This was just as well, because the next day he would be heading out to 'off-road'.

Lamb Timmis

Lambertus-Wilhelmus Timmis's mother was Dutch, and his father was British. He was brought up in Holland, largely by his mother, as his father was away from home most of the time, serving with the Royal Navy. In contrast to Choc, Lambertus-Wilhelmus had voluntarily taken the initiative to shorten his first name, once he had strayed outside of the Dutch territory and the confines of its unusual language, primarily in the generous spirit of improved communication.

Choc and Lamb had met at a motorbike shop in the capital. Having arrived in the shop around the same time, their egos had simultaneously been engaged in the same 600cc trail bike. It was the only one in the shop on that particular day, and probably the only one for sale in the city. The owner couldn't believe his luck that these two rich foreigners were fighting over a slightly dodgy second-hand bike rather than getting an independent mechanic to confirm for them why it was dodgy and second-hand. Instead of letting them bargain down the price, as was normal custom in such situations, he tried to get them to bid against each other instead. Choc and Lamb caught on to the shop owner's tactics and decided they were having none of it. After all, part of the fun of being a child in Feiquon was to believe in your total superiority over the locals. It was their moral obligation to con ignorant people out of things of higher value, and not the other way round. However, during the long and drawn out process of wanting a bike but not wanting to pay for it, it became apparent that Choc and Lamb shared a few mutual acquaintances in the biking fraternity. Eventually, they decided that neither of them should buy the over-priced trail bike, and go for a beer together instead to arrogantly exchange biker stories and to compare scars.

In between ordering beers and trips to the toilet, both men secretly phoned up Feiquon friends, whom they told to go and buy the bike for them at local prices, and there was a cut in it for them if they did. Subsequently, both of the biker's avatars arrived at the bike shop at the same time, and fought over the machine in question much harder than the two foreigners had.

For them, no bike meant no cut. The shop owner, being your average astute, financially aware shop owner, quickly worked out that the two foreigners had returned to bidding in his shop by proxy, and the price steadily climbed once again. Eventually, Lamb's 'second' was triumphant in the bidding war, and Lamb became the proud owner of a rather over-priced second-hand trail bike. Choc's initial resentment dissipated when he found out how much Lamb then had to spend on this new machine to get it working properly. Choc later bought himself a very different 500cc trail bike from another shop, having learnt from Lamb's 'mistake'. However, the event was the beginning of a strong friendship and a shared biker story. It led to some actual trail biking at the weekends and, over time, eventually resulted in the imaginatively crafted sign at the end of the street that read 'Choc and Lamb's Trail Bike Tours'.

Bush

Vince had not been outside of the capital since the start of his foreign adventure. Up until this point, his warped vision of Asia was based on traversing a section of the city triangulated by the hotel he'd arrived in, the market where he got his DVDs and vegetables from, and The Karot Rooftop Bar.

Much as 'off-roading' in the wild and untamed wilderness was a daunting prospect, in reality, getting safely out of the city without crashing had been the biggest challenge for Vince. Even in the early morning, the traffic was fairly full-on and crazy. Everyone but him knew where they were hectically aiming for. As someone who was only on his second brief go at riding a trail bike, Vince already felt he had enough to contend with, without the added challenge of other people zipping manically around in front of him and cutting him up.

The hard-nosed battle-ready bikers had met at 6.00am outside Choc and Lamb's, and greeted each other with various tired sounding noises and grunts, whilst shuffling around next to their monster machines with their hands in their pockets and kicking listlessly at bits of grit on the edge of the road. This ritual of tribal dialogue was to communicate that 6.00am was not their usual time, and that they had been out partying 'til late the night before' as per their street-cred requirements. To do otherwise and engage in using actual words or sentences would not gain the respect of their peers. They then noisily exposed the neighbourhood to a fifteen minute orchestra of five large trail bikes warming up. Short, noisy exhausts screamed with the pain of hot gases passing through the early morning chill, and kick-started engines rattled with anger while they were revved by their masters, who simultaneously chain smoked rough-tasting local cigarettes. Eventually, the pre-departure ritual was complete and one by one they started to pull down their visors and tear off at speed down the side road and towards the morning traffic. The biker convoy was led by Choc, and he was followed by Eriq, then by Pich. Vince was next, and Lamb brought up the rear to ensure that any 'stragglers', which was a euphemism for Vince on this occasion, didn't get lost or left behind.

Eriq was a genuine tourist and a genuine trail bike tour customer. He and his girlfriend had taken three months off from their usual office work in Toulouse and had headed for Asia. He had spent two months of being the intellectual and devoted follower of his girlfriend as they visited numerous art galleries, museums, temples and places of historic interest. He had dutifully tempered his personality to engage in concerns of architecture, culture, delicate sculpture, and traditional handicrafts and fabrics. However, Eriq had finally decided he couldn't cope any longer without regenerating his macho ego, and sent his girlfriend off to look in the craft markets and other boring tourist stuff for a couple of days on her own while he did something manly, for fear he was rapidly turning into a eunuch. There was currently a danger that he would return to France sounding a bit pathetic when describing the whole travelling experience to his drinking mates. He'd gained sufficient insight into the varying production methodologies, thread qualities and clothing design techniques in the cottage silk industry to start his own boutique, but not gained any biking scars worth getting out in public to demonstrate unquestionable feats of bravery.

Pich was the son of the large bike shop owner in town where Choc and Lamb had first met. His trail bike was a similar model to Choc's, but a lot newer and shinier. Vince assumed that Pich's father wanted to make sure that his son always got the best. If you have money then your neighbours need to know about it. The shop was also advertised on the fuel-tank and plastic fairings of the bike, so there was clearly an additional ulterior motive for Pich to be ripping noisily around town as part of a biker tour and drawing attention to himself.

After an hour of riding fearlessly through the fume belching and confusing traffic, the city started to dissipate from urban sprawl into flat agricultural countryside. Post-harvest rice farms formed a patchwork of cracked dry soil fields set within a mosaic of low earth walls, pinned down with sporadic coco-palms as they waited for the rains and the next planting season to return them to thick greenery. The horizon was peppered with villages of stilted wooden dwellings encamped within tall coco-palm palisades, from which generations had maintained the annual farming cycle.

The contrast between the bustling, hectic city and the

tranquillity of the rice plains was appreciated by Vince. He might have gone for a more profound analysis of the extremes had he found an opportunity to look up from the road for more than a second. The city's feeder-roads were a different experience to the urban chaos, but still had their considerable hazards. At this early hour they included children walking along the road on their way to school, two or three a breast with no care for the speeding vehicles they shared their route with. Vince had not yet developed the confidence to navigate his way past these moving and unpredictable obstacles at the same speed as the others. There were potholes to be dodged, dogs running out in from of him, pigs, goats, cows, and chickens running out in front of him, and people running out in front of him. He was amazed by the speed at which the front three bikers in the convoy had taken off, in light of this highly mobile and random obstacle course. There was certainly little opportunity to take in and enjoy the view with all of this going on.

For lunch, the trail-bike tour stopped at a road side café on the edge of a provincial town. After all of the straggling members had caught up with their leader, Choc, they found an outside tap and washed the thick patches of dust from their faces where their helmets had failed to shield them. The band of comrades took over a corner of the local noodle shop and ate large plates of fried rice and bowls of watery soup. As they returned to their mission, there was a short fuel stop and they refilled the tanks of their bikes. A kid at the side of the road with a wooden shelf lined with a variety of glass bottles sold them their petrol, taking the red-dyed murky-looking liquid one litre at a time and carefully pouring it in. Shortly after resuming their journey the convoy turned off from the paved and potholed highway and onto a dusty side road leading into the deep forest.

Vince quickly decided that the best place to be in a convoy of trail bikes on a dusty forest road would have been at the front. Otherwise the thick cloud of dust kicked up by all of the preceding motorbikes became a considerable challenge both in terms of breathing and seeing where you were going. Vince was not particularly prepared for these additional handicaps. His inexperience in staying upright on a bike in the first place seemed enough to be going on with for now. He therefore chose to hang back a long way to achieve a slightly more transparent vision of where he was heading. Lamb had pulled alongside him to share the track, so that he also avoided travelling behind in Vince's dust.

An hour later they turned off again onto an even smaller track. This time they were really out in the forested wilds. The twists and turns of the pathway helped the trail bike prove its worth amongst the dark and foreboding forest tracks that occasionally gave way again to lighter scrubby trees, and rocky outcrops. Shallow streams, small river crossings and damp feet were followed immediately by the smell of buffalo dung cooking on hot motorbike engines as they climbed the opposite banks, where the animals had also trampled their way to dry land post-wallow. It all combined to produce an energising of the senses and create an appreciation of realism and adventure. The shared damp smell was all part of the collective knowledge that they were pioneers in uncharted territory. Vince's thoughts turned briefly to his paranoid concerns that watching Hollywood movies had conditioned him with. Bandits with AKs would be lurking around every corner, waiting to take them to bamboo prison cages. Giant snakes would be curled behind every fallen log and vine-strangled tree, waiting to prey on him should he lose his concentration and descend from his bike into the undergrowth. Now that Vince was actually in the depths of the forest, it seemed that these phobias were fears that people in safe places chose to worry themselves about. Being out here in the jungle, being part of it, living with it, the dust, the sweat, the heat, the sodden shoes and the strong odour of buffalo shit coming from beneath the engine, the only focus was him and the bike, the excitement and the exhilaration, and the smell.

The Village

Dusk began to settle and the playful light on the gold-green leaves of the dry broad-leafed forest began to wane as the evening shadows slowly reclaimed their place amongst the cicadas. Vince, closely followed by Lamb, entered a small secluded village. Lianas gave way to coco-palms. Undergrowth shrank back to reveal the traditional stilted homes, fashioned from the wood of the surrounding jungle. Lamb accelerated past Vince, and then led the way through a small maze of tracks between the dwellings to a slightly newer looking wooden house on stilts on the other side of the settlement. The three other motorbikes had already parked-up beneath the house, and Choc could be seen on the balcony above, already with a beer in his hand.

Vince was exhausted. It was probably the most exercise he'd ever done in one day in his life. He had wrongly assumed that, unlike riding a bicycle, being on a motorbike took away the exercise element of two-wheeled travel. However, his arms, legs and shoulders ached like never before. He slowly dismounted, removed his helmet, and with a gait resembling that of John Wayne after a particularly long movie of chasing cattle hustlers across Texas, made his way delicately towards the ladder-like stairs at the front of the house. He removed his damp shoes, and wrung out the brown and odorous dampness from his socks. He then dumped them on top of his shoes before he climbed up to the raised floor where Choc was sitting in a rounded rattan chair and grinning. Eriq had found a hammock at the side of the room to relax in, and looked as though he'd already settled in for the night.

"The cool box is there, that small room on left side is where you'll be sleeping, and the bog's out the back. I'll grab you a cold one."

As Choc headed to the cool box filled with watery ice and tins of beer, Vince peered through the open doorway at the back of the house to the compound beyond. A little way back was an old hand pump next to which Pich had already stripped to his underwear and was in the process of taking a cold bucket bath.

Vince noted the small ramshackle wooden latrine building at the rear of the compound, next to some banana trees. His thoughts of snakes sneaking around in dark corners started to return, but he was soon distracted by the arrival of Choc at his side, who gregariously push a tin of cool beer into his hand.

"That should clear the dust from your throat, Vince."

"That was a great experience, Choc. I could do that every day. It's much better once you're away from the main roads and out on the small tracks."

Choc nodded in a smug and knowing manner. He was clearly pleased that there was a new convert to the fraternity, and he could claim credit for being the instigator.

"The woman I pay to cook will be here soon with the rice. The village chief will be round later for a beer as well, I expect. And probably bring his own fairly lethal rice wine with him as well. He'll be mainly after the scotch I promised though. I'll give you the tour while we wait."

Vince followed Choc back down the stairs to ground-level and then took on the unenviable challenge of getting his wet socks and trainers back on, before squelching after Choc to the back of the house.

"I had this place built by the villagers."

Choc proudly made a sweeping gesture with a thick arm to encompass his colonising progress, which included the house, a large shed and the en-suite amenities.

"Every few trips we do a shopping trip and one of us, Lamb or me, brings the Land Cruiser up here with supplies. It means that the cook can do different foods like burgers and steaks. It's also good to make sure the supply of beer, water, bog rolls, spares for the bikes and stuff like that never runs out."

"Can you not get toilet paper, and meat and that in the village, then?"

"The local suppliers are very good at some things, but not really meeting the home comforts that our holidaying customers are after. Besides, the return journeys with the Land Cruiser are always very helpful to us as well."

Following the final remark, Choc winked at Vince. Vince wasn't quite sure why. Clearly he was insinuating something, as that's what winking always indicates. That or you've run out of chat-up lines, or you're playing piano in a wine bar and trying to impress a girl at the end of the bar whilst performing a particularly tricky bit of the solo. The last two seemed by far the less likely of the options that Vince could identify. Of course, a return journey was essential if there had been an outward one, but that was blatantly obvious and not a breakthrough observation worthy of a sly wink. Maybe Vince had imagined it. It was getting dark after all. Maybe it was a reaction to a mosquito buzzing around Choc's face.

"Come on Vince, I'll show you round the storage shed."

Choc's grin became even more broad, impossible though that should have been, and he trudged off towards the large shed, expecting Vince to squelch after him. The large barn doors were secured with chains and a couple of large padlocks. Choc gave Vince a torch to hold while he fumbled around with a set of keys.

"You've got to be careful who you trust these days."

Choc proffered his wise advice as the final key turned the last padlock and some of the chains it was binding fell to the floor. He pulled the right side of the heavy wooden door open wide enough for them to slip inside and then he disappeared stealthily into the dark interior. Vince followed.

Choc observed Vince as his guest dutifully flashed the torch around the shed. It was as though Vince was on a guided tour of a dull cave, but was expected to feign interest for fear of the tour operator directing complicated questions about stalactites at him, and then shame him with his ignorance in front of the tour group if he got it wrong. As far as Vince could tell, the far corner did, indeed, contain a shelf with a few bags of toilet rolls and a few tinned supplies. There were also some bottles of oil for the bikes and what Vince could identify as brake cables and spark plugs. To the left of him were large bundles of what he assumed was fairly pungent tobacco, and to the right was a large stack of wooden planks.

"What do you think then, Vince? It's a pretty tidy set up we've got here."

Vince could sense a high level of pride in Choc as he surveyed his slightly uninspiring shed full of knick-knacks and forest products, and decided a positive response was expected by his host as part of this whole 'bonding over a shed' thing. Vince had never been much of a man's man, but he was aware that for those who were, conversations about engine parts, mechanics tools and indeed the sheds they kept them in were all part of crossing emotional friendship-cementing boundaries.

"Very nice, Choc. Good that you've got so many spares for the bike. You look very well prepared. That's a lot of wood. What are you planning on building out here next?"

"Na, that's not for wasting on buildings. That's Rosewood, Vince. You don't throw that away nailing up shacks in poor villages. It's far too rare and valuable. Sell that in the city though and it's worth its weight in gold. We usually fill the bottom half of the Land Cruiser with it and take it back into town. The police have never stopped us. They're too busy trying catch out vulnerable young women who've not got their moto's paperwork on them and extracting a few dollars as a bribe. They've not got the bottle to stop people like me. Anyway, I know a very wealthy and generous man who will happily take off my hands as much of that wood as I can bring him. Very discrete, if you know what I mean. The village chief sorts out the supplies at this end. I keep him in whiskey, cigarettes and a bit of spending money. All in all, it's a very tidy business. That's not what I've brought you in to see though."

Choc gestured towards the bags of pungent tobacco against the opposite wall.

"Now this stuff could be a nice little earner that you might want to get in on, Vince."

Forest products

It had been a while since Vince had been stoned. It had also been a while since Vince had sat with a bunch of blokes passing around bottles of hard liquor. A teenage party round at Shaun Lacey's place, where they'd downed three bottles of cheap Vodka and then rolled up because Sam Daley had scored a teenth was probably his most recent point of reference. However, add in the vaguely pungent and ever-present scent of buffalo excrement, and the rice wine, featuring some suspicious-looking submerged additions that had proudly been described to Vince as goat's testicles, and overall the evening could be considered as a bit of first.

Despite his chubby digits, Lamb was clearly no stranger to constructing a well-balanced joint. Vince had never had the patience for this and could never grasp the pride that others took in their art of configuring the skins and getting a tight roll. The chief was happily packing his weed into a large local pipe, but for the moment that looked even more dangerous to Vince, who had not arrived mentally prepared for sharing a bong.

The six of them sat in a circle on a woven mat made from dry grass, sharing their sitting area with the post-meal remains of watery soup, some limp and stringy pond-weed like greens, and a vast serving of rice acting as the centrepiece. The dim light-bulb hanging from the roof in the corner became a magnet for a large variety of moths and nocturnal insects as they flitted anxiously around it. The long shadows of the dinner guests were cast across the open balcony and into the scrubby trees beyond, where the cicadas persisted with their evening orchestra.

Of the three vices on offer, Vince tried to focus mainly on the scotch, hoping this would reduce the pressure to indulge too excessively in the other local products that were on offer. He'd been carefully monitoring the rice wine and in the two glasses that he'd received so far he'd mainly got a serving of cloudy alcohol and nothing more solid than that. As the bottle emptied, the probability of Vince receiving a grey marble of soft flesh was ever increasing. Meanwhile his cognitive ability to spot the arrival of pickled genitalia was continually being compromised with each additional glass. The chief had more sociable ideas about wine distribution than the other members of the party. Seated next to him, every time Vince took a polite sip of the local brew, his glass was immediately refilled with more of the musty offerings, whilst the chief cheerfully tapped Vince's knee and raised his own glass to his toothy smile to encourage a toast and ensure that Vince got totally wasted with him.

The evening's post-dinner conversation was predictably one that would not be suitable for mixed company. However, Vince was starting to see a lighter side to Choc and Lamb. As the night wore on, they completed gregarious tales of hijinks in expat bars, drunken exploits on river cruises, girls that Choc and Lamb had competed over, girls that Lamb had teased Choc for pulling, girls that had been viewed less favourably the morning-after in the cold light of day, and of course biker stories. They recalled daring feats of riding skill and speed, the occasional fall, and the inevitable comparisons of scar tissue and evidence of minor surgery, displayed as the trophies of adventure. Choc was quite the orator after a couple of shots of organ-flavoured home brew and could tell a good story. More than that, he clearly delighted in delivering a good yarn, and many tales had the well-hued fluidity of anecdotes that had been used to entertain many a traveller before. Choc was transformed from his usual and gruff shoulder-chipped self to the well-practiced host of a dinner party, making sure that all of the guests felt comfortable and of equal importance at the gathering.

It was much, much later in the evening when Vince finally crawled into the second room on the left, found a mat on the floor with a cheap mosquito net above it, and sank into the deepest of pickled testicle-induced sleep. This collapse into an exhausted alcohol fuelled hibernation was all the more satisfying, having just survived his first encounter with a basic rural latrine. Drinking a ruminant's marinated testicles may not be the most desirable past-time from a stomach-turning perspective, but it did seem to have taken the edge off Vince's anxiety towards exposing his vulnerability in a dark, enclosed space, which his paranoia had guaranteed was knee-deep in lurking reptiles.

The offer

The next morning Choc rolled up to Vince with a freshness Vince could only dream off. Vince's head was still fairly blurry from the previous night's pleasures. Also, his socks and trainers were still wet and cold from the outbound journey, so neither end of him was particularly inspired to crack on with the day ahead. Vince perched on the end of a wooden bed that was underneath the house next to his bike. He started the unpleasant process of squelching his feet into their damp and unpleasant coverings ready for the return trip. Choc walked over and sat down next to him.

"So, Vince, what do you reckon?"

"Reckon to what?"

"Getting in on the game. It's win-win. You can't deny the supply chain is well set up from here to the city. You, on the other hand, have your own rooftop bar. It's the perfect set up – all about the marketing."

"Choc, I don't think having cannabis in the bar is a good idea. Even if it is outside in the open air, people can still smell it."

"Well, I'm not suggesting that you write it up on the specials board, Vince. No. But you can become a local dealer. You'll get more customers for the bar as well once the word gets around to the right people. The Karot is the perfect spot. A few discrete packets supplied to well-vetted clientele, meanwhile you get a split of the profits and get to sell them a few beers as well while they're taking their delivery. We could all do quite nicely from it."

"Well, it sounds interesting, Choc. It's not something I was really expecting. Let me think about it for a bit."

Vince, with damp and unpleasant shoe installation finally achieved, summoned up the energy to bring out his motorbike from beneath the stilted house so that it was ready for the return journey. He was not at all sure that coming on this trip was proving to be the fantastic idea he had originally believed it to be. Yesterday morning he was an expat with a bar in the capital, who was looking forward to a trail bike ride. Now he was in the inner circle of a drug and precious wood smuggling ring, for which the trail bike business was a front, and he was expected to sign up as one of the dealers. He'd already been shown around the storage, and had even spent the evening smoking the product. Once you were in the know, and that deep in, it would be hard, if not impossible, to back out. Things were not working out quite as he'd hoped.

Vince noticed that Pich and Eriq were already starting up their bikes, so he thought he'd do the same. As he did so he noticed that Choc was putting on a large rucksack and then he gave a similar one to Lamb before walking over to him.

"Here you go, Vince, can you help us out by putting that on? It looks big, but it's fairly light. You won't notice it after a while."

Vince took the rucksack, feeling reluctant, but trying not to show that he was reluctant. He may have been a bit slow off the mark when he was first introduced to Choc and Lamb's other business, but he'd caught up with the situation now, and was under no illusions as to what he was carrying back into town for them.

Return journey

The journey home was an uneasy experience for Vince. He didn't know much about weed, but what he did know was that it was nearly always illegal. He also remembered that even a small amount of it was very expensive. Kids at parties used to pool together to buy a 'teenth', or a 'quarter'. These were very small parts of an ounce, which was also a very very small thing. Meanwhile, Vince currently had a fifty litre rucksack stuffed full of drugs secured onto his back. It must be worth thousands of pounds, or more.

Vince also knew that some countries' authorities were less tolerant than others when it came to the possession of drugs. Some countries had the death penalty for carrying drugs. In some countries you could talk your way out of punishment if you were cashed-up and knew the right people. Was Mr. Vanarith the right person to help with the 'talking your way out with some cash' method, for example? Could Vanarith talk his way out of a teenth or a quarter only? Could he be relied upon to explain away fifty litres of fresh bud if he had to? Where did his skills and his moral obligations lie when it came to a 'rucksack weight'? Clearly with such questions flying around Vince's head, he was panicking a little and it was starting to impact on his enjoyment of the return journey.

Towards the end of the morning the trail bikers reached the main road and ate at the same noodle stop as before, and then continued on back to Khoyleng. The second leg of the return journey gave Vince even more time to think about his moral and legal dilemma. This was mainly because Lamb had got frustrated with following him, and eventually flew straight past him in hail of revs, two-stroke fumes, and dust. Vince had understood that Lamb would be heading somewhere north that afternoon, and eventually peel off to a different highway, and not back to Khoyleng with the others. However, without a frustrated Dutchman on his tail, it meant the pressure for Vince to keep up was reduced a bit and his pootling approach to trail biking became more pronounced. It also meant that he would have the challenge of trying to find his way back to The Karot on his own, which added considerably to the pressure of his primary worry – which was the burden of becoming Feiquon's newest drug smuggler.

His relief at seeing the city loom in the distance and the margins of the highway become more densely populated with homes and roadside stalls was short-lived. Choc had said that roadside policemen tended to round up delicate and vulnerable women to extract minor sums from them before they could go cheerily on their way. Despite this comforting explanation of their terms of reference, Vince suddenly found that he was being flagged down by a uniformed officer, indicating to him that he should stop immediately.

The uniformed official motioned to Vince to put is bike at the side of the road and to get off. The officer then started talking quickly at him, which was totally incomprehensible to Vince. Vince's grasp of local vocabulary had so far centred on ordering beer and getting ripped off in the vegetable market.

"I'm sorry mate, my language isn't good. D'yaw know any English?"

Vince shrugged apologetically, to help demonstrate his inability to participate constructively in the conversation that the officer had initiated. The officer got out a document and started waving it at Vince, while his instructions seemed to get considerably louder and even more rapid. Eventually another officer wandered over and joined them.

"He want to see licence."

Vince was momentarily relieved to learn that the second officer had some English skills. He hadn't been sure how they were going to progress from the current impasse in the absence of even a few shared words, and he'd spotted that his vacant expression and continual shrugging had seemed to agitate rather than facilitate the first officer in his duties. His relief was short-lived when, having reached into his pocket to fish out the requested paper, he remembered that had didn't actually have a driving licence. It had never occurred to Vince that he would need a licence. He was quite sure that no one in Khoyleng had ever passed a driving test, making proof of doing so a redundant exercise. Also Mr. Vanarith had known he was off on the trail bike tour but hadn't offered to sort any paperwork out for him at a reasonable price. It was unusual for him to not spot an opportunity to raise a few funds with his document trade, and so this alone had confirmed to Vince that a licence was more of an extravagance than a necessity.

Vince was a rare recipient of moments of inspiration, but the increasing pressure of his doomed and immediate situation seemed to elicit one. He reached into his other pocket and dug out his wallet. From within the folds he eventually produced the forged Polish licence that he'd had made the year before when one of his trade-ups was working as a mini-cab driver.

The first officer momentarily studied the licence. Unimpressed, he passed it to the second one, who had spoken to Vince in English, mumbling as he did so.

"What this? Not licence."

"It is, mate. It's Polish, and valid internationally. I used it when I was a driver in England."

Vince's bold and indignant stance was ill advised. The police were looking to be cooperated with, not challenged in their observations.

The second officer looked back at him with a stern expression. Vince could sense that the tension had ratcheted up a notch.

"This is not international licence. Show me international licence."

Vince, having played his only card, inadvertently reverted back to shrugging like a simpleton.

The second officer held onto the forged Polish licence and started talking animatedly with the first. Vince was starting to panic. Not only did he have a fifty litre bag of weed strapped to his back, he was driving illegally and had just handed over forged documentation to an officer of the law. A document which the officer in question seemed determined to keep hold of, despite all involved having now agreed that its significance in the immediate discussion was minimal. Eventually the second officer turned back to speak to Vince.

"My friend here is thinking what to do. Maybe you can buy him beer to help him think."

Vince noticed he'd been pulled over just past a small stall, and pointed it out as an option.

"Maybe they've got one there, I can go and look for you, if that's okay."

The second officer shook his head, more with an air of pity than annoyance. Was this guy really that stupid? They were negotiating a payment, not planning to organise a night out together.

"Maybe he wants to buy his own beer. Maybe he needs a case of beer?"

Vince final twigged. Normally he wasn't one to submit to bribery, but as he had an enormous bag of pungent weed on his back it might be a good idea to indulge them on this occasion and facilitate a hasty exit. Vince produced a note from his wallet.

"There's twenty dollars here. That should help, I would think?"

The officer swiftly took the note and handed it to his mate, who grinned. This guy really was stupid. The officer was expecting negotiations for a box of beer to eventually settle somewhere around the two dollar mark. No one had ever actually given them enough for a crate each before.

"Okay, you go this time. But sort your licence."

The officer gave back the false Polish licence and Vince quickly pocketed it before shoving his helmet on and returning to the saddle. His speed quickened after that. If any other officers tried to pull him over he'd just have to pretend he didn't see them.

Escape

Around 8.00pm that evening, Vince eventually arrived in his street and parked the bike outside Choc and Lamb's house. If he'd presented himself as the embodiment of the gait of John Wayne the previous evening when he'd dismounted, then his current attempt at walking was probably more comparable to Wiley Coyote after a particularly unsuccessful TNT incident.

Vince pushed open the gate and wheeled his trusty charge into the front of the garage. Of course, all of the other bikes had long since been returned and were already washed down and parked up.

Choc appeared from the stairs at the side of the building.

"Vince, mate, you finally made it back then?"

Vince silently nodded. It was one of those observational greeting which were hard to respond to without stating the obvious yourself. Sophea, in a recent surge of confidence had started to try to initiate brief conversations with Vince using statements about his current activity. Opening statements such as 'Ah, you are wiping the bar', for example, tended to throw Vince off guard. It seemed there was an expectation to confirm that yes, he was wiping the bar, even though they both knew that it was clearly indisputable. Vince felt that proceeding down that route diminished their already limited communication rather than added to it.

Despite Vince's resistance to vocalising an assessment regarding his current and obvious progress in relation to the completion of his return journey, Choc persisted with the conversation anyway.

"How did it all go, you seem to have taken a while. Everything okay?"

"I was pulled over on the edge of town. Couple of police wanted to see my licence, but I've only got the Polish one from when I drove mini-cabs. In the end I gave them $20 and they sent me on my way."

Choc smiled.

"A bit of an adventure then, Vince?"

Vince nodded again. He was too tired to craft a conversation that would avoid further entanglement with the suburban underworld, so slipped off the rucksack and handed it over to Choc.

"I'd better get back to the bar. See how Sophea is faring on her own. Thanks for the trip, Choc. Really great. Good fun."

Vince turned and headed for the open gate. A rapid exit seemed to be his best chance of avoiding any further discussion for the time being. The last thing Vince needed right now was to be invited in for a beer and to hammer out the finer points of his up-coming and pivotal role in an international drug syndicate. To be quite honest, internally Vince was starting to become really worried. His grip on the situation was slipping through his fingers like spaghetti through a poorly designed colander. Choc, unaware of Vince's reluctance to communicate his apprehensions, took the rucksack and headed back up the stairs towards his apartment. After all, Choc's subconscious was well aware that the front entrance of 'Choc and Lamb's Trail Bike Tours' was not a renowned venue for deep and meaningfuls amongst its protagonists.

Back at the bar Vince found that Sophea was fully in control of the business of getting people sloshed. She had taken quite well to bartending. There were only a couple of customers quietly gazing at their drinks, and occasionally prodding a blunt fork into the top of slightly rubbery-looking lasagne in an investigative manner, so Vince decided it would be a good time to grab a shower. Refreshed, at least externally, he returned to the rooftop and contemplated his options over a glass of draft.

He started by reviewing the current circumstances:

He had agreed with Choc and Lamb, pre-departure, that there should be closer ties between The Karot and their own slippery dealings, Vince's understanding at the time was that this involved a cross over between guesthouses, bar meals and trail biking, and nothing else. However, Choc had taken Vince quietly into his confidence whilst they perused the inner sanctum of his remote village shed together. Vince was now aware of Choc and Lambs' business in terms of supply, storage and some elements of the outlet. Vince had watched enough movies to know that once you have that much inside knowledge that you're one of the gang, whether you want to be or not. Traditionally, there was only one way that it was possible to leave. Therefore, by default he was now technically a drug dealer. This seemed rather unfair, as Vince did not want to be a drug dealer and, indeed, other than being an unwitting courier, he had yet to deal any drugs. It complicated things. It was not something by which he was particularly driven and he had a very limited grasp of the system, other than a vague awareness from his teenage years of 'teenths' and 'quarters'. Mostly, however, he did not want to be breaking the law in a society where his capture was unlikely to give him the opportunity to serve in a low security environment and either learn a new trade or get a university degree before being returned, upgraded, to the free world filled with renewed prospects. The consequences here were real. Vince had run away from things before, and on the face of it, there was no reason not to do exactly the same thing now. Well, actually there was. It was much more difficult to run away in a place where you couldn't speak the language and barely knew where you were, let alone where to run to. However, overall this brief review gave Vince a focus on which to concentrate his pounding and panicking heart. It was not a question of what to do, just how.

As is often the case, the third and quickly downed glass of draft seemed to bring the answer. His distraught mind had momentarily drifted off to thoughts of Maly in an attempt to become calmer. His initial thoughts had centred around an overall need for a bit of comfort and someone vaguely sensible to talk to. He started wondering whether he had been premature in abandoning her as a romantic option. Their first date had gone okay, but he had sensed a general level of incompatibility in terms of their levels of spiritual enlightenment, and this had deterred him from pursuing her further. Vince had been scouting for a good looking local girl to call is own. Maly seemed to be interested in socialising with a foreign friend, but also wanted someone to talk to about her church. Vince's desire, or indeed ability, to join what was effectively a scripture focus group had not been high and his need to pursue her company had waned proportionately.

It was as Vince's current reverie of the delightful girl began to take hold that he observed that Maly was one of the few people he knew that had geographical experience outside of this particular slice of downtown Khoyleng. Vince knew that her boss at the teaching school ran a hotel in the coastal town of Dhokratt. He could offer to work there a while. Make out that he was doing research to scale things up at The Karot, but really lie low long enough for Choc and Lamb to forget that Vince was supposed to be a drug dealer for them. Then there was the church where Maly did voluntary work up in the north somewhere. He could go up and volunteer to do things. People did. Often TV showed that do-gooders would arrive at such places for a few weeks, saw wood, nail things, initiate structures and then leave having captured the lifelong adoration of the unfortunate people whose lives had been eternally revitalised by this brief interjection of woodwork. Vince could go and nail stuff together. They probably wouldn't turn him away as that wouldn't be a very churchy thing to do. Again, Vince's absence from The Karot and Khoyleng could be easily explained by a desire to impress a cute local girl with his GCSE woodwork skills. This would elicit a response from Choc more along the lines of 'way-hey' than the 'what about our arrangement for you to be principle dealer of our drugs' line, and again buy Vince some time for things to blow over.

All of a sudden, Vince had options.

Maly

Maly hadn't seen Vince socially for over a week. Their last encounter had been when they'd had lunch together. She could therefore be forgiven for being a little unprepared when he turned up on her doorstep at 9.30pm looking a bit shaky and walking like he'd had an unfortunate incident with a well-sprung trampoline. At their last meeting at the riverside restaurant she had wondered if perhaps she had been a bit premature in telling Vince all about her voluntary work with the church and what she believed in. She noted that some people reacted in unexpected ways when they heard her talk about her religious connections. Vince had given the impression that he hadn't really followed and understood what she was explaining, so maybe he was in that category as well.

Vince hadn't given a clear reason, but had explained he wanted to get out of town for a while. Maly didn't think it was so strange. After all, at the language school she worked with a lot of expats travelling through who wanted to seek out new experiences. Many of her temporary teaching staff decided that they'd arrived in a paradise where anything goes and normal rules didn't apply. Subsequently, she had also observed that a number found themselves in situations where they needed to vacate town in a hurry and not discuss this with her in advance so that she could have the opportunity to re-schedule their classes. Therefore, it was more unusual that she was actually being informed prior to the departure of one of her part-time staff, rather than being left to work this out after they'd failed to show up at the school.

Vince had presented Maly with two options for his future that he believed she might be able to help him with. The first was to work for Frank Schneider and his wife Wendelin at the hotel on the coast. To be honest, this was a non-starter, as Maly's original banishment from the hotel was strongly linked to the unpredictably jealous tendencies exuded by Frank's bratwurst-loving wife. Doing favours for Maly that would reach the attention of his significant other was not something that was going to benefit Frank, and 'Frank's benefit' was always the main criteria for Frank deciding to do anything.

Option two, volunteering at the church, was therefore a much more do-able option if these were the only choices. Maly had phoned up Pastor Matthew to explain that she was despatching a new and enthusiastic worker, and that he should expect Vince to arrive in Maklai town the following evening. She then wrote down the travel instructions for Vince both in Feiquon and English. She used both to provide multiple resources to enable him to negotiate for this seat on the early bus the next morning. After that, Maly wished him luck and promised she would also be up in Maklai Province to visit in the next few months and looked forward to seeing how it was all going.

Vince had left Maly's small apartment building and returned to the street outside the residence a much calmer individual than when he had gone in. There's nothing like smoothing the stress of an immediate and dangerous situation with a hair-brained and impulsive solution. Vince's current gung-ho ad-hoc resolution was so random it had been written out for him to follow in two different languages.

Trainee Pastor Matthew

"If your faith is in yourself, who will have to pay the penalty for sin?"

Vince stared quizzically at the pastor as he pondered earnestly over this unexpected observation. The pastor beamed back at him with the sense of pride of one who had come up with a clever question, but failed to be compassionate enough to allow it to remain rhetorical. To be honest, Vince had no idea at all what the answer was, and wondered if perhaps the question was probably a bit hard for him.

Vince had envisaged that he would primarily be a short-term participant of the church community. Mainly he had hoped he would be allowed to generously devote time to nailing planks of wood together, but without the expectation that he was there to actively commit to becoming a graduate of spiritual philosophy.

In contrast to the pastor's question about the penalty for sin, paying the penalty for 'crime' was a topic that Vince had deliberated over at length in recent days. Specifically, the national penalties for the crimes of drug smuggling, illegal trading and logging. His conclusion was that he had considerable faith in the authorities' ability to take great care in ensuring that the penalty of crime was paid for. This was not something he was able to take comfort in. Meanwhile, Trainee Pastor Matthew was coming at the subject of 'paying penalties' from a very different tangent. Vince couldn't quite see the connection between 'faith in yourself' and 'penalty for sin', or why it should be so high on the conversation list between two men who had only just met. Football, or the relative pros and cons of the British Royal Family, for example, were staples of uncomfortable early gambits between British travellers and new foreign acquaintances, but this had so far been completely overlooked by the reverend. Under the circumstances, Vince figured it was easier to go just go along with it, and so nodded thoughtfully in the direction of the trainee Pastor, hoping that physical acknowledgement of the deep and meaningful observation would cover the immediate social need for a response. Pastor Matthew, taking this thoughtful response from Vince as a positive sign, decided to give an opinion of his own on the conundrum.

"Before I came here, I only had faith in myself. I worked in Khoyleng, like you. I had a business and I made a lot of money. I was a very successful man. Then I learned about the church, I was trained, I came here. I saw my error in loving money and I found faith. I changed by name to Matthew."

"That's very interesting Pastor... Er, well done."

Vince was delighted to realise that Pastor Matthew had no idea about the answer to his own question either, and so he didn't feel quite as inadequate. The pastor certainly hadn't touched on the sin element of his riddle, and the faith bit was all rather vague as well. Vince was a little confused by the need for him to completely change his name though, and where that all fitted in. Vince hoped he would not have to change his own name as part of the forthcoming involvement in faith-based carpentry. For the moment, he couldn't imagine who else he would be, apart from 'Vince'. The trainee pastor was certainly not shy in striking up uncomfortable conversations, so Vince figured an explanation about the name-change would come with time, without him having to initiate it. Vince had made quite a few radical trade-ups of his own, but he'd never gone to the extent of changing his name. That was real conviction to a lifestyle choice.

Vince took the opportunity of the lull in philosophical reasoning, to change the subject:

"Perhaps you could show me the church, Pastor Matthew? I'd be interested to see it, like. You know, see what I'll be helping to work on."

Pastor Matthew grinned again. He motioned to Vince to begin walking down one of the village tracks, and once Vince had set off he followed just behind him. Being put in the lead when you're the one that doesn't know where you're going is not the easiest or more logical of tasks, but fortunately the distance to the new church was not too far from the pastor's house and after a few glances over the shoulder to make sure the direction Vince was taking remained acceptable, the new large building became apparent from behind the coco-palms.

The church building was a concrete structure. Ironically for Vince, it was the only building in the whole village that wasn't made of wood. Vince realised he would have to turn his hand to the masonry end of the construction industry fairly quickly if he was going to contribute meaningfully and justify his stay. The time that he'd made a table-lamp stand in school from a few bits of wood and a light fitting would provide limited tangible experience with which to guide the villagers in building concrete structures.

Pastor Matthew pointed to a water well that had a handpump fitted to it. It was positioned in the grounds at the front of the building.

"This is the borehole that the church provided, where the village can now get their water. We built the chapel nearby so that we can always be thankful for the clean water. Our faith is like water. It keeps us healthy and clean, it gives us life and drives out the impurities. These are the things you must have in your life so that you can have true happiness, Vince."

Vince nodded thoughtfully. Conversations with Pastor Matthew didn't seem to get any easier. He should also probably try and think of something clever to say as well before too long, so that the Pastor could see he was making an effort.

"That's very interesting, Pastor Matthew. So does everyone in the village go to church now, and sing hymns and that?"

"We have services every week on Sunday. We try our best to help the poor. This church is new, but it is not just for this village. The congregation will eventually come from the neighbouring villages in the surrounding hills as the word spreads. It is our duty to go and visit the people of those villages and help them to learn about faith."

Vince nodded thoughtfully. He could see that this new direction he was on would require quite a lot of looking serious and nodding thoughtfully. It would be a level of commitment to his neck and eyebrow muscles he'd never called upon previously.

Village work

Since arriving on the bus at Maklai, and then getting a moto-taxi to the village, the sentences written out for Vince on the scrap of paper by Maly had stopping being particularly useful. Pastor Matthew could speak English to a reasonable level, but he was one of the few. However, a number of the new congregation were trying to learn English. This was mainly because the texts from which the Pastor was trying to educate his community were in English. As they were fairly complicated, open to interpretation, and peppered with old fashioned phraseology, translation into a language where an exact version of a foreign word was sometimes difficult to pinpoint provided a further challenge. In this case, 'learning the language' had taken precedence over 'lost in translation'.

Shortly after Vince had arrived, trainee Pastor Matthew had explained that the wood for the new community building next to the church wouldn't arrive for a week or so. Therefore, Vince could help teach language skills to those who were interested.

Finally something was going right. Vince had met with a small group of villagers inside the new church building and provided some instruction in the art of speaking English. This was something in which he had recent experience and a certain level of confidence. His brief was to teach English. Luckily for Vince, he had not been told to do this by teaching the religious texts, as he would have been rather out of his depth. He figured if he provided some basic training in language using the usual methods from his time in Khoyleng, then his students would have the tools with which to figure out the gospels on their own. Pastor Matthew would no doubt be on hand to support them when the time came.

As luck would have it, the church had two rows of benches, so it was easy to set up his small language group in a two-team layout using the front pews, so that it was very similar to the set from *Family Fortunes*. He'd learned from his nan that using this game was a very adult-learning centred approach to language improvement. The added realism that pews and a lectern brought the game show meant that the early morning English course was a big hit in the sleepy community. When not teaching, in line with the ambience he was getting from his new environment, he spent his day suspended in a hammock beneath the pastor's house, dozing, pondering his current situation, and wondering how things would be different if Maly had come with him.

Vince's fourth day in the village began with his usual English class and he concluded his early morning routine with a game of 'guess the animal in English from the noise'. This turned out to be far more difficult than Vince had imagined. For example, Asian pigs don't 'oink' and frogs don't 'ribbit'. The lesson had rapidly deteriorated into an opinionated session on animal noise interpretations, as opposed to a class in which any actual English language was taught. Having considered the possibility that chickens might sometimes go 'kouk' instead of 'cluck', the debate over whether ducks go 'quack' or 'pip-pip' had dominated much of the second half of the session.

Just as Vince and his tutees were really starting to get to grips with a cross-cultural, mutual agreement with regard to the various nuances of goat mimicry, Pastor Matthew entered the church. He waited patiently at the back for the farmyard debate to acknowledge his arrival. Vince quickly wrapped up the lesson and walked to the back of the church to join him.

"Interesting lesson today, Vince?"

The pastor's opening had started off as words of encouragement but somehow become a question by the time he'd finished. Vince furrowed his brow and nodded thoughtfully, as he was now conditioned to do.

"We're starting with very basic stuff first. Besides, this'll make it far easier on a Sunday when you get as far as Noah's Ark."

It was the pastor's turn to nod while he thought of a response. Vince was pleased; he was clearly getting the hang of these deeply reverent conversations.

"Vince, I'm heading out to one of the nearby villages today. Perhaps you'd like to join me?"

Vince leapt at the chance. He'd spent four days in a small rural village where his main achievement had been establishing that it was difficult to have an international agreement of an acceptable impersonation of a water buffalo, and Vince was ready for a change of scene.

Outside the pastor had a small moto, and he invited Vince to ride pillion. Vince had off-roaded before on small tracks through forests interspersed with paddy and villages. However, that had been on a larger motorbike, one with suspension, and he had been the one steering. The advantage of being the principle rider was the ability to anticipate and make almost sub-conscious allowances for the bumps, pot holes, sudden swerves around buffalo shit, and other random hazards. Sitting on the back, you just had to take the jolts, the bangs, and unavoided animal waste as they came.

An hour or so later Vince disembarked from the bike with a different kind of pain than the one he had experienced on the trail bike. That had been a mix of muscle ache, exhaustion and adrenalin, which somehow combined to create an imprint of excitement as well as pain. Getting off the back of a moto as a rural passenger was just about the excruciating pain.

Having dusted himself down, Pastor Matthew was greeted by the village chief and they were both led up the steps of a stilt-house. They sat down on a woven bamboo mat near to an open window. The room was very airy and Vince looked out at the rest of the village and studied the layout as the pastor talked to the chief. He watched as the people went about their business. Children played, grandparents baby-sat, parents occasionally passed by the house and headed out towards the fields. Vince appreciated that the pastor was here to do good things, but he did start to wonder if the village really needed him, as they seemed to be doing okay on their own.

Meanwhile the pastor and the chief continued to talk. Vince was almost nodding off when Pastor Matthew announced it was time to leave.

"How'd it all go then with the meeting with the chief?"

"Good, Vince, very good. The chief and his family will come to see us on Sunday. It is very exciting. The head of the church in Khoyleng will be very pleased."

"Quite quick though, isn't it, Pastor Matthew? A meeting like that, and then for him to become interested in the church? I'd have thought it would take longer to get people to become interested. You must have explained it very well."

"These are villages with traditional beliefs. They believe in spirits. We believe in spirits, and demons as well. People have to follow rituals sometimes to appease these spirits, and so do we. The people think that their troubles are fate, but the animals that need to be used for rituals to pacify the spirits are very valuable in these communities. It is not easy to control the spirits. Luckily, we also have ways to drive away the spirits and demons without having to sacrifice animals. So, it's not so different really. It's not so strange that the chief would want to learn about this."

Vince nodded sagely. The pastor was drumming up trade like a door to door sales man, selling his church to the villages by helping them see the economic benefits. The pastor continued:

"Besides, the young people in these villages are starting to be aware of new and modern ways of life that are different to those of their parents. Why not have a new, exciting religion too?"

Vince started to suspect the pastor was starting to use his door to door technique on him as well. He decided for the moment that all of his mental strength was needed to prepare him to get back on the moto for another hour of agony.

As they took off down the road the pastor shouted over his shoulder to Vince:

"We'll have go back to our village now. We can visit the other villages further along this road next week. I'm expecting the first delivery of wood for construction of the orphanage. It's very exciting. The leaders of the church in Khoyleng will be very pleased with the progress."

With that the pastor sped off down the track with greater enthusiasm and less awareness of animal waste than on their initial journey.

Vince was surprised at this new information. He had thought they were making a community building. The pastor must have got his English mixed up. However, Vince gave it no more attention as he was a having a small epiphany of his own.

Vince's epiphany

This was actually the second epiphany that Vince had produced during his lifetime to date. The first intuitive leap of understanding had been the original trade-up idea. It had been a real break-through of an epiphany which had changed his entire life. He'd stuck to it with limited wavering for about a year and a half now. In a modern world of rapid change and innovation, that kind of commitment to anything was quite an achievement, and it was the reason Vince's previously dull and menial existence had rapidly become varied and colourful.

On the basis of past epiphany experience, Vince was delighted to realise he might be in the process of having another one. An hour perched at the back of a wobbly moto on a bumpy road demands a certain amount of staying awake from the pillion passenger. This requirement is in response to the effort to physically endure the pain of the hard saddle ceaselessly bashing into your hind quarters. There is also the challenge of following the flow of the moto with every sudden swerve prompted by the result of unrestricted pastoralism and animal husbandry being practiced on all highways, so that you don't fall off. However, with the challenge of this necessary awakeness, combined with nothing really interesting to do in its event but try to avoid taking deep breaths during very dusty bits, Vince's mind began to wander.

The mind-wandering starting point was his contemplation about the life choices of Pastor Matthew, the back of whose head was inevitably taking up a certain amount of Vince's immediate vision and therefore concentration. Vince had noticed that much of the pastor's motivation to rush around converting highlanders to his chosen direction of spirituality and the building of rooms in which this conversion could be followed up, was based on his strong desire to please others. He had purposely chosen to stop following his own selfish materialistic goals to take what he believed to be an alternative direction. However, in procuring this new philosophy, the pastor seemed to be obsessively trying to impress his spiritual supervisors back in the capital and beyond. He was focused entirely on what he believed to be the wishes of his sponsors, or even his supernatural mentor, but not really doing things based on his own decisions. To Vince, this loss of decisive control would be a problem for him should he venture down the same route. As he thought more about it, he realised it was actually a problem he already suffered from, more than most.

Vince realised, as he inhaled the fine dust of a passing moto, as they clattered past each other down the track, that he was always trading into someone else's life or philosophy. This meant he was trading into someone else's decisions and planning. It didn't originate from him. None of it did. Like the pastor, he was doing a job that it suited someone else for him to do, primarily as a piece in their bigger picture; overall it was for their advantage rather than his.

The Karot guesthouse had started off as Fairchild's inheritance-playboy scheme of owning property in Asia so that he could boast to his friends, and further ingratiate himself with his blood-sucking wife. Even though this scheme was later abandoned due to Fairchild's desire to pander to the twisting whims of his blood-sucking wife, none of these decisions were really anything to do with Vince or Vince's personal career plan. Vince had jumped on the bandwagon at the time, as it was the only real choice he had if he was to avoid slipping back to the bottom rung of the ladder again. Even now, post-Fairchild, The Karot was owned by Mr. Piseth the landlord. Even if Piseth had no interest in it for the present he could make future decisions without Vince, and all could suddenly change. At the language school, Vince was working to produce linguistically improved labour for beach-side German-owned hotels. Sharing the delights of the English language with people who couldn't get a low paid job without it was not Vince's personal dream or ambition. It was merely a device for Frank Schneider, to enable the wrath of his terrifying but significant other to be spread more thinly, and for Vince to score some extra cash. Meanwhile, he was in the back-end of nowhere, inviting the onset of dust induced lung disease as a result of his entanglement with Choc Cadby. This was certainly not the outcome of beginning his life-plan with a blank canvas and the working out what was best for Vince. The epiphany was clear. Vince had to turn things around, and become his own boss. Genuinely this time. The trade-up plan still stood. His unwavering commitment to better and better trade-ups remained. The next trade-up though, needed to be one where he was truly his own master. He had to stop running from Choc. He had to stop being a means to fulfil someone else's goals. Vince had to take charge for himself.

Construction

Pastor Matthew pulled up outside the church building. Vince peeled himself from the back of the moto, dusted himself down, coughed up the rest of the dust he'd been inadvertently gathering, and then vigorously rubbed the back of his legs to try and get some circulation going. The pastor, meanwhile, almost skipped his way to the other side of the church in excitement to inspect the arrival of the wood. Vince stiffly made his way to join him.

A small truck was parked up and couple of the younger lads from Vince's language group were helping to unload planks and lengths of wood into piles at the side of it.

"So the community building will go there then?"

Vince gestured in the general direction of the wood. He'd worked out that when the pastor got excited the conversation got complicated, so he was better off being the one to start any dialogue between them, and focusing on something fairly down to earth and manageable.

"Yes, yes. The orphanage. We have to wait for the concrete footings that the columns will sit on, and then we can move ahead with the first part and work on the frame."

The pastor excitedly moved to the truck to direct the unloaders to do what they were already doing, in his desire to be an immediate part of the whole thing.

Vince mentally confirmed that it was to be an orphanage then. The word had been used twice now, and with a certain degree of commitment. He was surprised to learn that there would be so many orphans about in these remote rural communities to justify an entire orphanage. He'd not seen kids begging at the roadside like there were in the capital. Having been to a couple of villages now, and seen the way families and communities worked together, he'd assumed that most of the time the extended family found ways to offer support if something happened to a child's parents. Obviously he had been wrong. Vince had no parents to speak of himself, and he had been brought up by his nan. He was certainly glad about this, despite his nan's short-comings, and would not have exchanged his early life, for all of its problems, with an institutionalised upbringing.

That evening Vince sat with the pastor for dinner. As usual, the staple was a large bowl of rice. They sat on the floor and began to eat. Vince decided to ask more about the new building, starting by trying to understand how many of the local children were orphans. From the way Pastor Matthew began his response, it sounded like a question he'd had to answer before.

"The orphanage is there to help poor children who have no parent to care for them. There are many orphanages like this one. Some of the orphans have no parents, some of the orphans are children whose parents are very poor and so cannot care for them. Having the orphanage means that they can bring them here where we can help them. They will be much better off. There are plenty of volunteers like yourself who are passing through and help them with food and education."

Vince didn't really follow the argument. He sensed that a difficult spiritual question would be posed if he pursued it further, and he knew he didn't have the mental capacity right now to follow it. However, Vince was even more clear now that this was not the place that he needed to be. Earlier he'd had his epiphany about being master of his own destiny. Staying with the pastor and building an orphanage for kids that weren't technically orphans was so far from his epiphany that no amount of stretching could conceivably connect the two. Vince decided he would change topic and explain his epiphany instead.

"It's been helpful coming here, Pastor. It's given me time to think about stuff. When I was on the back of the bike this morning, I realised I need to take a bit more control of my life. You know, be in charge of what I do, rather than helping others to make money."

The pastor nodded thoughtfully.

"Sounds like it was your fate to come here. There is a purpose in everything. It's like Jonah. He ran away, but eventually was helped to realise that he needed to return and face his responsibilities."

Vince was impressed. The pastor's ability to turn around a general comment about life into an analogy of a children's Bible story at the drop of the hat like that was quite a skill. The pastor wasn't quite finished:

"Maybe you should change your name to Jonah."

Like Pastor Matthew, Vince had gained his church name after all.

Dentistry

Nigel Salmon's battle-axe receptionist had voluntarily resigned from her post of intimidation in the end. Fay Clarke did not like Nigel Salmon one bit. He was too wet. All limp handshakes and effeminate posturing. He was constantly apologising for himself. Not a real man at all. His very existence grated on her nerves, whether they were in the proximity of the same building, or she was on her annual get-away in the Canaries with her sister. The very fact that he still existed never ceased to annoy her, to the ruination of every foreign holiday. She had long since resolved that she would not be beaten by this. Why should she be the one to give up her career and income just because of the existence of this babbling excuse for a boss? If she persisted with the stalemate long enough, eventually he would sell his practice to a proper dentist and move to a different part of the country to grate on someone else's nerves. She knew she was wearing him down. The man was increasingly becoming a total wreck. In recent years he'd looked considerably more unkempt and dishevelled, and would even stumble over words when he talked to her. This obviously made him even more irritating as time went on, but the end would eventually justify the means. Soon there would be a new man in charge. One who cared what people thought of him, a well-dressed man with a business-like attitude that she would admire and respect. It was all just a matter of time.

It was to Fay Clarke's dismay that, just as she was on the brink of crafting the final stage of Nigel Salmon's mental obliteration, Natalie arrived. The proverbial spanner in the works had knackered Fay Clarke's plan like a plague of wasps in a plum orchard. The blighted fruits of her labours were no longer there for the picking. Nigel had been transformed overnight into a proud, well-groomed man of confidence and charisma. Despite years of devious manoeuvrings and deep seated hatred, Fay was almost able to concede that Nigel Salmon had become slightly less insufferable. However, Natalie Sedgwick was on a whole different plane of antagonistic, skin-crawling frustration. Once Natalie had started hanging round the surgery, hooting loudly at Nigel's weak jokes and failing to dress appropriately for a woman of her age and figure, Fay Clarke knew that she had finally met her match. Nigel, on his own, was not sufficient reason to abandon her well dug-in position, but Natalie's arrival proved to be all too much. The battle-axe decided it was finally time to make a move.

Natalie immediately took over as receptionist at Nigel's surgery. She soon discovered that it was a job she loved. She had found her calling. Firstly, she got to greet new arrivals like an old friend from behind a bar-like desk. It was a skill she had honed over many years at the Carrot and Jam Kettle and so she took to it like a duck to water. The clientele also appreciated the friendly change to the dental reception, and it turned out many of them were more fearful of Fay Clarke than they had ever been of the dentist's chair. Natalie enjoyed other elements of her new-found career as well. She enjoyed talking on the phone and making appointments, managing the bookings and the payments. She also appreciated the free dental care. Her teeth had never sparkled so much. Most of all, though, she enjoyed taking the patients through to the dentist's room where her handsome and successful professional man greeted them with kindness and authority, and helped to solve their problems and ease their pain.

Natalie even took night classes with a view to becoming a dental assistant. For the first time in her life she felt she had meaning and direction.

Maklai

As had been the case with Maly when Vince had been initiating the outbound element of the religious carpentry trip, Vince had also asked trainee Pastor Matthew to write the bus ticket instructions down for him to support the return journey. Vince felt that this was more of a back-up plan this time, as he had picked up a few phrases since arriving in the country, and felt that getting to the capital was an easier task than leaving it in search of an obscure backwater village. If nothing else, he felt he should at least be able to recognise the capital as the bus entered it, which had not been the case when he first arrived in Maklai.

One of his new language students took Vince from the village and into the town centre on the back of a moto. He dropped him at the bus station next to the market in the centre of the provincial town. Vince then successfully negotiated the ticket for his seat, and established which bus he was supposed to travel on. It wasn't due to depart for a couple of hours and so Vince had time to wander past the end of the market and over to the noodle shop to organise a soupy breakfast before the long journey back.

Vince stared at his noodle soup and swished at it a bit to try to work out what the odd looking floating bits of meat might be. He also wondered how he was going to successfully consume the liquidy breakfast with only two chopsticks to help him. He peered across to a fellow breakfast souper a few tables over to see if he could get any tips by observing their technique. Instead he was just left wondering how his neighbouring diner could make such loud slapping noises with his gums whilst consuming such a watery soup. It wasn't like he was trying to consume wallpaper paste or help a live squid negotiate its way into his digestive tract. If anything, processing the soup was closer to drinking than eating, and so there should be limited need for anything beyond the most basic of skills. A combination of sticks and gum slapping as a means to facilitate digestion suggested that there was a general need to revisit the system. Perhaps this distinction between food and drink was where the apparent confusion lay.

As Vince was observing the noodle soup phenomena, he realised that behind the soup consuming diner, on the other side of the road, in front of a hotel was the off-road motorbike that belonged to Lambertus-Wilhelmus Timmis. The distinctive go-faster stickers of red-flame along the tank that Lamb had added in his attempt to customise his ride so it looked even faster, were unmistakeable. Vince did not need to be reminded that he had come to Maklai specifically to hide from Choc and Lamb. This, combined with the realisation that the two hours remaining before the bus was due to leave would be insufficient time for him to eat soup using only chopsticks, helped Vince decide it might be astute to leave the open exposure of the noodle shop. He would skulk around in the dark market alleyways instead, rooting around for any nutrition-free snacks to take on the journey.

As he stood to leave the noodle shop, Lamb strutted out of the hotel on the other side of the road, and made his way towards his bike. Lamb had a strong instinct to protect his bike as if he were a parental water vole fiercely defending its young brood from an unwelcome mink. He therefore had a sixth sense when it came to unwarranted interest in his pride and joy and could immediately fixate on anyone within a 200 metre radius who was looking at it. This protective instinct was a bit of a contradiction for Lamb as, in contrast to his parental urges, his ego also demanded that lesser souls should be encouraged to look on endlessly and drool in envy at his monster trail bike. Somehow he managed to psychologically resolve these conflicting emotions and, as he did so, he caught sight of Vince standing up to leave the noodle shop across the road. It was like two Wild West adversaries who had been previously unaware that they were so closely in each other's presence, and were now having the sudden realisation that the town was no longer going to be quite big enough. Lamb and Vince stared at each other across the road.

Fortunately for Vince, when he panicked it actually took a while for his facial expression to change to one displaying panic, largely due to the temporary shutdown of his entire nervous system, brought on by the panic. On this occasion the delayed reaction bought Vince a bit of time, and by the time his face was ready to take on an expression befitting the severity of the event, Vince realised that Lamb had already developed his own facially expressive look of panic. The two men stared at each other for a bit longer. Lamb continued to look panicky. The added confusion of this meant that Vince's nervous system still hadn't arrived at a conclusion, and he continued to remain devoid of any facial expression. Lamb, eventually out-psyched by Vince's apparent lack of emotional reaction, turned on his heels and headed back inside the hotel. Vince, both puzzled and relieved by the result which had avoided the need for any verbal communication or explanation of his presence in Maklai, quickly headed for the anonymity of the market.

Wendy and Lamb

Lamb had genuinely been caught off guard when he saw Vince across the road. The last he had seen of Vince was when they were heading back to Khoyleng with Choc and the others. Lamb, meanwhile, had peeled off from the convoy to head for Maklai for a few steamy days in the well-developed arms of Wendelin Schneider.

For Lamb, it was the perfect set-up. His woman was married and wanted to keep their liaison secret. This meant that Lamb had no obligation to commit to monogamy, which, in turn, meant that when back in Khoyleng and hitting the town with Choc, the 'anything goes' philosophy was in no way undermined by his clandestine liaison. Meanwhile, Wendelin had started her own provincial-town hotel business, which meant a steamy covert affair was well within the realms of possibility. It also had all of the benefits but none of the overheads. He had free board, free food, and free access to the bar next to the reception. Even free laundry. He'd actually considered only coming up every third week, so that he could bring enough washing with him to fully justify the petrol cost. It was win-win all the way. That was, until you were discovered by the idiot-kid that owned the roof-top bar in Khoyleng across the road from you, who lived with his nan.

Since returning inside, Lamb had watched Vince's movements from the hotel window. Vince had gone into the market next to the bus-stop. Lamb decided that he would continue to monitor from the window to see when Vince came out and where he went. He was probably waiting for a bus, as nobody came to stay long in Maklai. Most of the people using the hotel were there for one night while they waited for a connecting bus service to leave the following morning. Vince's presence was inconvenient and Lamb would just have to be more careful next time. There was really no harm done, yet. But if the idiot kid started bringing up Maklai in public then it could get difficult. Lamb frowned so that his forehead crinkled to form contours like a map of the grand canyon. He didn't like anyone being able to hold something over him. He didn't like it at all.

Wendelin lay in bed, staring up at the ceiling. She couldn't be happier. Lambertus had come to stay with her for a whole week. There was nothing to do but lounge around in bed and enjoy life with her muscle-bound hunk in an air-conditioned, mosquito-free room. Nothing that was, other than to call the maid to bring her the occasional selection of cold meats, cheeses, wines and bratwursts. It was as if her pitiful life with Frank Schneider and that slutty receptionist of his had never existed.

Back at The Karot

Vince had only been gone for about a week. It felt like much longer. Whilst it was a sufficiently long period to amass a wealth of experience on the spiritually variable aspects of foreign travel, it was a barely noticeable absence in terms of the passage of time that would be required for people to forget that you were working for them as a small-time drugs dealer.

Vince sat at the bar and stared into his glass of beer. Last time he had reviewed his worries about illegal shiftiness he had come up with options. This time, the only option that he had available to him seemed to be going along with it. At least that was the case for the time being. Epiphany number two and the self-determination dream would have to start by incorporating a more stable solution to his immediate concerns about operating outside of the law. After all, it would be difficult to become his own boss whilst he was under the control of a small time drug-lord.

"Vince, you look like a wet weekend on a pissin' bank holiday."

Vince looked up to see his nan hoist herself onto the bar seat next to him with her usual disregard for elegance.

"Yaw'm back I see. What was it like in the pissin' countryside, then?"

"Yeah, it was alright."

Vince had no desire to enlighten his nan further. Whilst he was fond of her, she had never been a person he could bring into his confidence and share his feelings with."

"Anyway, what's been happening here?"

"Well, your mate Choc, with the motorbikes, has come up with the goods, for a start."

Vince decided to take genuine note of his nan for a change, as she produced a rolled up cigarette from behind her ear and lit up. The sweet distinctive scent of the roll-up was reminiscent of a recent biking tour he'd been party to.

"I've not toked on anything this good since the pissin' '60s, Vince. Choc says there's plenty more where that came from an' all. Let me know if any of your mates want any and I'll sort them out. Me and Choc's got a deal going where I get free samples if I can drum up a bit of trade. He said he mentioned it to you, but you didn't seem keen so he thought he'd ask me instead. Mr. Vanarith's even partial to a drag himself, and thinks there's potential for a nice little business."

Vince had not expected this dramatic turn of events. If he had foreseen this, he would not have bothered to run away for a week and become spiritual carpenter. Thankfully, however, it did seem to make him redundant as a local drug dealer, as his nan had quite clearly staked a claim and taken control over what would have been his patch. Vince was relieved momentarily. He then started to wonder what the legal implications were of allowing your own nan to deal weed from your rooftop bar. Maybe that was one for Mr. Vanarith to sort out. One thing was clear to Vince after all the distractions of recent weeks, it was time to take trading-up his life seriously, epiphany style. His brief emersion into the world of the devout had at least led to a second life-changing revelation about doing stuff to feed your own dreams and no one else's. Vince now had clarity of vision and his immediate problems were behind him. Things were about to change.

Chapter 4 – Tuk-tuk

Entrepreneur

The key to starting a sustainable business is to provide people with something that they will always need on a regular basis. To Vince this was an obvious starting point. 'People will always need bread' was the sort of platitude that people like his nan would come out with, and they were probably right. Although, in his current environment the better analogy would be that people would always need rice. Sadly rice farming wasn't necessarily one of Vince's transferable skills.

On the other hand, the key to starting a profitable business is to encourage people to part with their money for something they think they really want, but probably don't need at all. This second approach also made a lot of sense.

Vince decided that in an ideal situation, a good business should somehow achieve a bit of both: meeting a regular need and also addressing a non-essential want. He realised that the two elements of thinking you want something, and actually needing something, didn't have to be particularly related, so long as they were both in there somewhere. A bit like Twiglets at a drinks party, where somehow the host is convinced they are both needed and wanted in preference to the many alternatives.

It was a strong beginning to business analysis, and was as far as the foundation for Vince's new business plan had got.

From his lookout position on the balustrades of The Karot, Vince stared down at a knackered looking tuk-tuk as it pootled down the street, gently engulfing an old lady in a puff of black smoke as it did so, while she pushed her handcart along, collecting used plastic bottles for recycling. Tuk-tuks were everywhere, and along with motos they were the core public transport system for the city. Vince wondered if there was a way to make some money out of them, and began to apply his new business theory of combining 'need' and 'want' to the tuk-tuk game.

The more basic of the human needs required to achieve subsistence included food, drink, shelter, and clothing. The next level would include security, knowledge, social wellbeing and so forth. Vince decided to concentrate his argument on the basics. His train of thought was as follows:

People *needed* food for nutrition and therefore survival. Whilst the need was quite clear, from Vince's analysis, what people actually *wanted* was to avoid sitting at a dinner table with their families, having mundane conversations which could lead to falling out and arguments. As a rule, the modern generation also preferred to be entertained by cookery programmes rather than wanting to participate in cookery. It was also preferable to avoid the effort of thinking about what to have for dinner, as this would lead to realisation of a lack of ingredients, cooking ability, and motivation. Therefore, over the millennia, subtle adaptions had gradually evolved to address the struggle between needs and wants. The resultant business solution to the need for basic nutrition had led to the development of a preference to queue up in a fast food restaurant to avoid cooking and unnecessary conversation, and to whittle down the complications of choice to 'with or without cheese' and 'one burger or two'. Vince very much put himself in this generational category of evolutionary achievement, and recognised that fast food was never going to be just a fad. It was an evolutionary pinnacle that not only fulfilled the wants of the masses, but also addressed the basic human need. Well sort of.

Drink was another basic that people couldn't survive without, and a glass of tap water had that completely covered. However, despite the regular availability of tap water, what people wanted, according to Vince's observations, was to rehydrate themselves at expensive coffee shops. This was so that young mothers could get out of the house and arrive in a place that had similar amenities to the house they had just left: coffee, chair, table, bathroom etc. However, the additional 'want' being satisfied was the ability to park up and compare expensive pushchairs with other mothers, and assess who was winning at the best mum contest by achieving an entirely aseptic living environment for junior to develop in. This was obviously then undermined by lining the infants up in the posh and expensive pushchairs at the coffee shop so they could all dribble in each-other's direction and exchange air-borne communicable diseases. Of course, for non-babied people, the primary drink option was going to a bar, which could often result in dehydration, rather than meeting the actual need to quench a thirst, if the participant got too carried away. From this analysis of needs and wants, it could be seen that there were clearly a lot of contradictions to overcome when developing a strong business plan.

The need for shelter had led to the needs of the masses being addressed by a want for a complex estate agent system of condos, duplexes, conservatories, extensions, house-chains and gazumping. The need for clothing was addressed by the want for high street fashion retail and a desire to pay inflated prices for bits of cloth stitched together, which helped the wearer compete with other people who also had the same competitive nature.

On this sound foundation of analysis, it was time to consider the business aspects of the tuk-tuk. The need to be addressed was to travel from A to B without wasting too much time. The current tuk-tuk design was a small cart with seats either hooked up to a moped or incorporated directly into the back of the motorbike itself. It was therefore a good example of something that hadn't progressed far beyond addressing just the need. However, the lessons that the examples from Vince's analysis had shown, was that the real money was there to be made once the business had addressed the 'wants'.

There were two main 'wants' that Vince could identify, that it could be argued that the tuk-tuk currently tried to meet. Firstly, having some form of carriage was an advancement on just riding on the back of a moto, so that people could travel in small groups without a family of four or more participants trying to concertina themselves onto the same motorbike saddle and still achieve mobility. Secondly, the passengers at least, although not necessarily the driver, were marginally less vulnerable to rain as long as the downfall wasn't too heavy and the tarpaulin curtains were properly maintained. Clearly, having only achieved two 'wants' so far, there were many other wants to be addressed before the tuk-tuk reached any kind of evolutionary pinnacle in the business world.

Vince decided that technologically, the tuk-tuk was as physically advanced as it was going to get. Any upgrade on the design and you'd be better off scrapping the whole thing in favour of a small car or a functional underground rail network. Investing significantly in either of these options was currently beyond Vince's finance capacity. The business niche to focus on then, was not the need of getting from A to B, but to address the inevitable time-wasting aspect of doing so. Vince, in an unusual move, applied some lateral thinking and decided to adjust the problem analysis accordingly. In reality, a genuine reduction in time-wasting could only be achieved by building a faster tuk-tuk and teaching an entire city how to drive properly and follow the road rules. What he needed to address was people's desire to believe that the period of time that they were spending in the tuk-tuk was not being squandered (rather than 'time-wasting' itself, which Vince astutely observed was quite a different thing, and something that people often quite enjoy doing).

Vince made a number of decisions. Firstly, he would buy a fleet of five tuk-tuks and paint them brightly, in a way that made it clear that they were a specific fleet providing a unique and very different service. By doing this, people would start to know that they were flagging down their ride for something a bit special. Secondly, the tuk-tuks needed to provide something that people did actually want to spend their transit time doing, in order to feel that it had not been squandered. Therefore, each vehicle would be installed with two DVD players and a large flat screen TV. During the daytime, one player would show a recording of the previous night's Asian soap opera, featuring women whinging in a high pitched voice about various domestic and relationship concerns, and the other would show a recording of a news channel or a documentary, should someone with sensitive hearing get picked up. Each could be switched on or off according to the nature of the clientele. In the evening, these DVDs would be exchanged for karaoke videos, again with a choice, depending on preferred style and the language in which out of tune warbling was required. Additional speakers, microphones, kitsch lighting and drapery to beautify the inner-carriage went without saying.

Initially, Vince considered that there would also be a set rate for services, clearly displayed on the side of the tuk-tuk, and that the charges would be based on distance travelled. The moto would even be modified so that the clock that showed the kilometres travelled could be glued to the inside of the carriage area. However, Vince quickly realised that whilst this innovation in setting the fare addressed a reduction in time-wasting, it wasn't necessarily perceived as something his customers would want. For many, a good use of time was engaging in the joy of haggling incessantly over the price, so this idea was quickly abandoned.

Finally, Vince decided that the back of the tuk-tuk would be used to advertise both the TV aspect of the service, and also The Karot Rooftop Bar. There would be a fifty per cent discount on the first glass of beer at the bar if the passenger could prove they'd used the 'Tuk-e-oke' service to get them there.

Organising the purchase of tuk-tuks and converting them into 'Tuk-e-okes' was fairly straight forward. He had already decided to opt for the moto-drawn carriage design. This would at least give the impression to Choc and Lamb that he was vaguely retaining a motorbike interest, albeit on a slightly different scale. Vince checked out how to get hold of a few good ones from Pich, his compatriot from the off-road trip, whose father owned the motorbike shop. Pich was now a regular at The Karot, so it was easy enough to catch up with him. His father didn't sell tuk-tuks, as he was targeting the cashed-up foreigner off-road enthusiast with his particular enterprise. However, he was in the motorbike business and a couple of contacts further down the chain, and Vince was ready to make his investment. The Tuk-e-oke business would address the wants of the masses whilst inadvertently satisfying a slight need.

HR

One good reason for Vince to get into the tuk-tuk business was to have an excuse not to get into the off-road business. By going down this route, Vince had achieved the additional advantage of distancing himself in economic and legal terms from Choc and Lamb's underhand dealings. He therefore made it a priority to explain his new tuk-tuk business venture to Choc and Lamb, so that they could also quickly but indirectly arrive at the same conclusion. In many ways, Vince was starting to get the hang of the culture and the art of misleading understatements.

As always, Choc had an opinion. Vince had assumed Choc would pontificate about the unimpressive size of a moto compared to his macho big-man bikes. However, he was actually more opinionated about the HR and driver recruitment side of things.

According to Choc, expats usually bought motos as a gesture to quell the truculent brothers and close relatives of new and exotic girlfriends, whose family were sceptical towards expats. This was a way of buying your way into the parents' good books, and playing your part at wealth sharing across the extended family. It was better to engage early on in the wealth equalizer system. Normally in society, anyone who got ahead was expected to redistribute their advantage amongst the less well-off family members, thus preventing the over-achiever from reinvesting their new capacity for improvement in themselves, and taking their advantage any further. By showing your reinvestment hand early on at a moto level, they were better placed to argue against providing the long term loan for the metallic painted SUV request from the family when entrenched further into the relationship, and the family economics of marriage were under delicate negotiation.

Vince appreciated Choc's astute advice. Largely because it meant that Choc hadn't picked up on Vince's subtle diversion from further participation in the off-road illegal smuggling caper. However, in the absence of either a new girlfriend or a recalcitrant friend-in-law, the challenge of identifying employees through this 'two bird with one stone' approach remained problematic.

As he didn't have his own extended family, Vince decided to advertise for tuk-tuk drivers. He got Sophea to translate a simple advert, and sent her out into the streets to photocopy it and then stick it on walls and the equivalent of lamp posts. A week later, despite the arrival of five shiny new tuk-tuks in the street outside The Karot, Vince had not received any applications for the position of driver. Essentially, the flaw in Vince's advertising plan was that the people in the town who had time to stare at job adverts glued to back-street walls were either people who couldn't read them, or tuk-tuk and moto drivers lazing around between jobs who already had their own tuk-tuks and motos.

Plan number two was to encourage the people he knew to get involved. Perhaps it was a good opportunity for them to help out their own extended family members, but without the expense. At least then the new drivers would have references. This turned out to be a slightly more successful strategy. Sophea said she would see if her younger brother was interested. Mr. Vanarith had a friend from one of the document processing offices he liaised with whose daughter needed to find some work.

The third man to join the driving team was called Mr. Oudom. Sophea had found him asleep in one of the new tuk-tuks as she arrived at work one morning. His apparent affinity with the vehicle seemed to make him an ideal candidate for the job, so she woke him up and took him inside so he could sign up.

Within a week the Tuk-e-okes were ready to hit the streets. They were painted up to display both The Karot Rooftop Bar, and the additional multi-media service. All DVD players, DVDs, speakers, microphones, kitsch lighting and drapery to beautify the inner-carriages were in place. It was time to hit the streets.

Tuk-e-oke number one. Vichet

Vichet had been hanging out with his mates at the end of their street when Sophea phoned him to tell him he had the job. At the time he decided that the message from his older sister was fairly good news. One of his friends had just got a new mobile phone that had a far better ringtone than his, and he was showing off about it quite a lot. Some extra cash might help Vichet to get one up on his mate. He could buy a really good new phone if he managed to not immediately spend what he earned on glue and alcohol.

For Vichet, there were other advantages to the tuk-tuk job, beyond the obvious promise of ready cash. Tuk-tuk driving was not like a normal job. For a start, quite a lot of the day could be spent sleeping in the back of the tuk-tuk. There was a comfy seat, shade, and you could put your feet up. As long as you parked up somewhere that you couldn't be monitored by the boss, then no one could prove you hadn't just had a quiet day and that it had been hard to drum up any business. Another added value was that he could arse about with his mates in the tuk-tuk, and drive them to places, probably shopping centres, where they could hang-out and try to attract girls by sniggering at them and making rude comments. It also might help him to keep his mum and dad off his back for a while, and dampen their repetitive complaints and whining about the hours and company that he kept. Vichet accepted the job immediately, and Sophea passed on the good news to Vince.

Vichet was the younger brother of Sophea. However, having heard the news of her boss's business expansion into transport management, it was not just a sense of sibling love and devotion that motivated her to push his name forward. Vince had not expected this from Sophea, as she had never been one for expressing emotions – be it passion, anger, or even vague passing interest in what was going on. The sudden arrival of an opinion after all these months meant that Vince couldn't help but take it seriously. Sophea had pushed for Vince to give Vichet the tuk-tuk driving job and Vince had responded.

Sadly, whilst Sophea had spent much of her life being

pushed by her parents to be responsible, and was expected to find work to support the family, her brother was the spoiled little prince who got to hang out with his mates, dodge school, be arrogant and rude, and latterly sniff quite a lot of glue. By the time their parents had realised what a useless child they had allowed to evolve, and that they probably shouldn't have paid off the teachers so that he could pass his exams, it was far too late to take any corrective action. Sophea's motivation to see her brother in the tuk-tuk job was to get Vichet away from his dodgy glue-sniffing mates and on the path to a more responsible life.

Vichet was never going to be convinced by this responsible philosophy. However, a Tuk-e-oke could mean that he would be able to work and still hang out with all his mates. Maybe he would get some extra cash, but mostly he would sit in the Tuk-e-oke singing along loudly to the DVDs and showing off to girls, and sniffing glue. The motivations of him and his sister were therefore extremely different, but not completely irreconcilable in terms of the tuk-tuk stewardship. Vichet decided he would give it a try.

Vince had started to look on Sophea in a distant extended family kind of way. Therefore, following Choc's observation about dishing out motos to truculent family tearaways, this was as close to supporting a relation as Vince was likely to get. Unfortunately, the problem with dishing out random motos to truculent family tearaways, was that the investment was largely a means to impress a girlfriend and gain the financially motivated blessing of her parents, an unlikely spin off would be a marginal reduction in wayward tearing by the truculent. It was rarely done with a view that a responsible employee would immediatly emerge from the gluey fumes.

It took only one day for Vichet to write-off the new Tuk-e-oke.

For millennia, the perceived way to impress girls has been to demonstrate speed. Some of the fairer sex may not agree with that philosophy in all situations, however, being the fastest in a race, zipping about on a horse, or floating around whilst displaying rapidity in a seal-skin canoe, is a key part of every hunter/provider's résumé when eliciting a mate. On the streets where Vichet competed for peer group attention and a tally of benign giggles of approval from girls who should know better, it was all about riding a moto as fast and out of control as you possibly could. This included weaving and swerving dangerously in and out of the traffic with the misguided assumption that, out of all the other unschooled motorists navigating the crowded streets, you were the only unpredictable one. Clearly, on taking receipt of the new Tuk-e-oke, the exact same principles applied.

Sadly, Vichet had never driven a tuk-tuk before, only a moto, and he found two key differences. Firstly, as two young moto-ists found out to their cost, the tuk-tuk was wider than a moto and didn't fit in the space between other motos like his old motorbike used to. Fortunately, the traffic lights turned to green only a few moments after he had pulled up in the middle of the two unfortunate travellers, and sent both of them and their vehicles to the floor. Vichet was able to pull away while they were still picking themselves off the road and so the consequences were limited. His three glue-fumed mates in the back thought it was great, and encouraged him to provide further entertainment.

Having eventually reached what Vichet considered to be an impressive speed for dangerous weaving through traffic in a tuk-tuk, he got the opportunity to learn that it was difficult to lean a tuk-tuk into taking a tight corner. This became very apparent to him as the motorbike and carriage scraped dramatically along the road on its side with the momentum and unwavering persistence of an enthusiastic spaniel that thinks it might be on the scent of something which may or may not have passed in the general vicinity sometime during the previous three days. Vichet and his mates scraped along the road with continued speed: Vichet trapped under the moto, his mates bouncing along the bitumen through the open side of the carriage, which had since taken over the role of the floor of the compartment.

The scraping was short-lived, as the machine rapidly connected with the exterior of a glass-fronted sea-food restaurant. By the time the sideways tuk-tuk began to slow from its journey's deviation, it was already about two tables deep into the dining area. The overwhelming confusion, raining shards of glass, displaced rice, high-pitched hysteria, floods of salt water, and rapidly escaping herds of octopuses were just part of the chaos that ensued. The police quickly arrived on the scene to assist their relatives in the looting of unsupervised lobsters. They then un-wedged a mangled Vichet from beneath his mangled ride, and packed him off to the hospital. This, of course, was on condition that he paid the fare to get there, and then reported back to the police once he was better so that they could arrest him properly.

The Tuk-e-oke was probably a write-off, as was much of the seafood establishment. However, unlike the owner of the 'Lucky-Lucky Sea Food Restaurant', towards which the police displayed a degree of sympathy, as he was an influential mate of their superintendent, Vince was informed that the damaged Tuk-e-oke would be impounded indefinitely. It meant that, from a practical perspective, the tuk-tuk was never going to return to its intended function. This was very much in contrast to the tribe of seven octopuses that had made a pact to join together in their escape by working as a team to negotiate the open sewer system. By the time Vichet was admitted to hospital, they had already reached the open river and were sitting in a row on a large piece of driftwood heading for the high seas. From there they agreed that they would separate, and take their chances on their own to make the long journey back to their families.

Sophea was devastated at the news of the accident, mainly due to her embarrassment that she had talked Vince into letting her glue-sniffing idiot brother to be in charge of anything. Secondly, the brother's demonstration of such total ineptness was not going to relieve any of the parental pressure for her to be the high-achiever in the family. Not only did he lose his tuk-tuk, but Vince ended up having to pay for Vichet's hospital bill, otherwise this responsibility fell to Sophea who couldn't afford it. It had not been her best move in terms of impressing the boss.

Tuk-e-oke number two. Ms. Chantrea

Ms. Chantrea had finished secondary school a few years earlier. Even though her father had strongly supported all her teachers, the expensive piece of paper she received at the end of her education was only going to help her until her employers realised that the document didn't match very strongly with reality. Should she start a job that was achieved on the basis of her qualifications' misleading recommendations, it would soon become apparent that her abilities were lower than indicated.

Regrettably, she wasn't cut out for anything academic, or anything that involved more than basic literacy. Her father did not own a business that she could become part of. However, over the years he had managed to progress a few steps up in the government office where he'd spent his career pushing paper around. So, although the family couldn't afford for Chantrea not to go to work, her father's pride and standing in the office meant that he couldn't let his family status slide back within the space of one generation to doing menial jobs like cleaning. There is a linear scale, where everybody and every family fits in society. You are either higher or lower than your neighbour, but never the same, and it's only sensible to make sure all movements of status are upward. Chantrea's father was therefore faced with a considerable dilemma.

Mr. Vanarith happened to be passing by the office of Chantrea's father to organise part of the paperwork for a new factory, which needed to demonstrate the environmental impacts of the enterprise had been thoroughly assessed. Somewhere along the line, Mr. Vanarith brought up the topic of the Tuk-e-oke. He felt it was a shame that a new tuk-tuk was on offer, with no wayward family members for him to recommend to snap up the opportunity. Chantrea's father decided that because the Tuk-e-oke was something that Mr. Vanarith wanted in his family, although he lacked the pre-requisite youthful relative needed for the venture, then it would be good enough for an actual existing youth within his own family. Also, as the Tuk-e-oke was no ordinary tuk-tuk then, at least superficially, his neighbours could be persuaded that being its pilot would be less socially embarrassing than if his daughter became a cleaner or even the driver of a normal tuk-tuk.

From Vince's perspective, there were a number of clear disadvantages when it came to employing Ms. Chantrea as his driver of Tuk-e-oke number two. Firstly, her father would only let her drive the tuk-tuk between the hours of 7.00am and 5.00pm. He was very strict on this point. Chantrea was an unmarried girl from a respectable family of civil servants, and being out in a tuk-tuk in the evening would damage her unblemished social standing irrevocably.

Secondly, she wasn't very good at riding a tuk-tuk. The traffic scared her and so she generally tried to avoid the busier parts of town. This meant that she avoided most of the potential customers as well. The passengers that she did manage to pick up tended to then get taken on very tortuous routes around the outskirts of the city in order to get to where they were going.

On the up side, Chantrea had made her own personalised additions and modifications to the carriage area. This focused on the installation of numerous garish fabrics hanging throughout the roof and seating area. From these were attached a multitude of fluffy dangly creatures designed to bounce around in people's faces like giant flies that had been genetically crossed with particularly kitsch aliens. Although these additions were slightly surreal to begin with, Chantrea had decided there was even more kitsch-ness to be achieved, and carefully cut holes in the back of the heads of the obscure fluffy characters, and then threaded in fairy lights, two per creature, before sewing them back up. Having eventually found a place where the fairy light wiring could be twisted up with the wires for the DVD player to make them flash on and off, the creature's eyes lit up in a variety of random and disturbing colours when the karaoke was playing. She also hung up a number of air-fresheners that combined their chemically derived fake essence to achieve the scent of fruit rotting on a hot vinyl car seat that's previously been stuffed with damp pine cones. So, from a kitsch and a 'not your average tuk-tuk' perspective Chantrea was at least getting with the programme.

Sadly, the start of her employment coincided with the beginning of the rainy season. Presumably, long before the invention of Tuk-e-oke, there was a time when the drainage system of the capital matched that of the infrastructure and habitation which it was designed to serve. However, over time the urban plots had been filled with multi-storey blocks of flats, and patches of open ground had been concreted over to ensure the new SUVs didn't get their four-wheel drive mechanisms muddy. All of this development had been done very much at an individual level, and was facilitated by the likes of Mr. Vanarith, who made sure that the paperwork and signatures flowed in a timely manner, so that the advancement of the built environment never lost its impetus. The public works and infrastructure needed to support these developments, and notably the city's drainage, had failed to keep pace. Of course, the outflowing of liquids from one property investment is very much the problem of the next person downstream, rather than a concern of the owner himself. Subsequently, when it rained there was a sudden arrival of an immense volume of water, that had few options in which to drain away. After a particularly intense downpour, a considerable number of streets, particularly those away from the main thoroughfares, would rapidly accumulate water that had nowhere to go, other than back up into the sky once the sun came out again and helped it to evaporate. Finding yourself somewhere between knee and waist deep for a couple of hours during a storm event was not uncommon.

The very fact that Chantrea avoided the main roads while performing as a tuk-tuk pilot was fundamentally linked to her eventual undoing. It was late afternoon and she had picked up a group of elderly ladies who were dressed up in their best silk and embroidered finery. They were on their way to a wedding, and had embarked into the Tuk-e-oke just as the first spots of rain splashed down on the canvas roof, descending in tandem with the gathering winds. Chantrea predictably chose a tortuous route of backstreets to ferry her aging passengers to their required destination. Despite their frailty, her charges still had to endure the loud karaoke, whether they wanted to or not. This had been the case for all passengers ever since Chantrea had rewired in the scary creature light bulb faces using her trial and error approach to reorganising the electrical system. The storm quickly raged to near typhoon proportions, and Chantrea was battling through the torrential downpour. The streets were awash with water, and SUVs surged past, drenching her and her charges with copious volumes of spray in their wake. Chantrea could barely see where she was going through the deluge and so, in her panic, decided to take an even more obscure route than usual. The rain-drenched roads hid the potholes from view. She clattered along the streets, her vehicle crashing violently though the hazards that she could no longer avoid. Before long she was hopelessly lost. One rain-drenched side street was much like another and she peered through the pelting rain, her clothes soaked through and clinging to her delicate frame, her drenched and matted hair sticking to her wet face, her eyes stinging from the impact of the heavy water drops as the wind whipped them furiously around her. From behind she could make out the desperate moans of her miserable itinerants. They huddled in the middle of the carriage in a futile bid to keep their costumes dry, further frustrated that this survival option increased the range and effort needed to spit beetle nut out into the road and the furious storm beyond. Eventually Chantrea exited a small street at speed in a haze of vapour, as the wheels slipped and skidded through the water-soaked thoroughfare. As she did so, Chantrea found that the tuk-tuk was flying uncontrollably into the middle of a cross roads where she sloshed to a sudden halt. Normally this would be a busy junction that would take an age to edge the nose of the tuk-tuk into until her progress was such that the cross traffic had little option but to let her continue. However, on this occasion Chantrea was very much on her own in the junction, with the flooded moto sitting marooned in at least two feet of water. In contrast, the four elderly but well-dressed women behind her were only sitting in about half a foot of water. Onlookers in stranded cars further down the street observed Chantrea's dramatic entrance and eventually felt the gentle wake of water her tuk-tuk's arrival had created as it made its way stoically along the street and sloshed apologetically against their radiators.

 Chantrea didn't realise that it was possible for a fire to start whilst sitting on a motorbike, whilst it was broken down, and in a small lake, and in a thunderstorm. She had assumed that the vast amounts and different sources of water involved in the current predicament, along with the degree to which both she and the bottom portion of her current passengers were drenched, would make it entirely unlikely. And yet that was what happened. The combination of her enthusiastic rewiring encountering a damp environment, and the highly flammable content of kitsch cuddly toys with red-hot light bulbs that had somehow remained fairly dry as they bobbled around without mercy in the upper-reaches of the carriage, meant that the carriage roof area was the first part of the unlikely contraption to fire-up. The intensity of the inferno was to such a degree that no amount of spitting beetle nut at it was going to bring it under control. Chantrea desperately tried to restart the moto, but to no avail. The panic of the elderly red-teethed women behind her was intensifying. They didn't know whether to destroy their outfits and submerge themselves into the cold flood waters, or take the risk of their coiffures going up with the ceiling fire. Beetle nut was getting in short supply. As she tried to entice the women from their indecision, Chantrea was surprised at just how many people were prepared to come out of their shelter and into the downpour to stand around and watch as she helped four angry old ladies from their burning carriage and navigated them slowly to shore. There is a fine line between audience and entertainer, but today it was Chantrea's turn to experience the latter. By the time her charges were safely on higher ground at the other end of the street, the rain was easing off a little. Chantrea could see that her tuk-tuk had drawn quite a crowd of inquisitive onlookers, admiring the height that the flames achieved as the searing heat engulfed the remaining coverings, TV screens and seat cushions, and the fire was whipped higher with each new gust of unforgiving wind.

An hour or so later the waters had subsided enough to enable the remains of the gutted machine to be pushed to the side of the road. Mr Vanarith had answered the frantic call from his colleague's daughter, and once the tuk-tuk was pushed out of the way he had taken her back to her mother so that she could recover from the ordeal.

The four drenched elderly women had also made their way back home, once they had worked out which obscure corner of the city they were starting from. They immediately got changed into their back-up finery of silk and embroidery, and took a real taxi to the wedding hall, just to make sure that they got there this time. They were two hours late for the event, but decided they hadn't really missed much. At least they had a bit more news than usual to share with the other guests as they eventually tucked into the shrimp-based hor d'oeuvres.

Tuk-e-oke number three. Mr. Oudom

Mr. Oudom was a retired gentleman. 'Slow and steady, and slightly drunk' was his over-riding but rarely communicated philosophy on most things. And get in a good nap if you can. It was an approach that had worked well for him when he had been a security guard outside the district administrator's residence in Jakmee, right up until the point that they'd had their first break-in. The burglars got away with most of the administrator's possessions, including his award for badminton, presented by the now retired Provincial Governor, as Oudom had been too slow, steady and drunk to raise himself from a good nap to do anything about it. Clearly this semi-successful approach to medium-term employment would also work in the tuk-tuk trade, until the first thing that went wrong. At which point he would apathetically look for another lowly position which he didn't mind losing either. In a similar vein to the truculent Vichet, Oudom also identified tuk-tuk-ing as an occupation which, if managed sensibly, could include quite a lot of not doing very much. As he'd been originally recruited because he'd been napping in one of the tuk-tuks, Mr. Oudom felt that his new employers would not be greatly concerned if his continued work-ethic reflected this apathetic approach. It would also provide somewhere to sleep at night if his wife was going through one her phases, when she nagged him unnecessarily about drinking away all the money she got from selling plastic kitchenware at a stall on the outside of the market.

Vince had interpreted Oudom's 'slow and steady' demeanour as 'responsible and reliable' and Sophea's translations in the interview didn't seem to contradict that.

For about a month Oudom carried out his duties with limited controversy. He wasn't bringing in a lot of money, but he had delivered quite a few unwitting customers to The Karot, a number of whom had returned on several occasions. From that aspect of the business plan strategy, Oudom was working out quite well.

It was when Oudom's sister fell ill that things changed. She lived in the provincial town of Maklai, which Vince had also visited briefly when trying his hand at spiritual carpentry. Word had reach Oudom via one of his sister's friends that she was mainly bedridden these days, unless there was something interesting on at the temple.

Fortunately by now, Oudom had built a four to five hour siesta into his daily work schedule, from about ten o'clock in the morning onwards. He parked up beneath a shady tree in a quiet back street, reclined in a comfortable position on the padded seat of the tuk-tuk and stared up at the sky between the leafy branches to ponder. His sister had sent word to Oudom that she was ill and needed him to send money to her to help buy more medicine. For Oudom, the local medical situation was a bit of a paradox. When he himself was ill, he'd happily seek extravagant levels of funding to acquire traditional healing, massages for his back, suction cups to bruise his chest, plasters on the temples, any random herbal remedies that could be found, and whatever unmarked concoction of colourful pills a medical practitioner in a white coat suggested to encourage him to part with his money. However, when he had to fund another person's indulgence in multi-faceted health care he was a little more sceptical about where his money was going. It would be so much easier, he thought to himself, if he was living there with her.

By 2.30pm Oudom had decided that he should definitely be up country with his sister so he could keep an eye on her. Besides, tuk-tuk-ing was easier in the provinces, there was less traffic to have to concentrate on and avoid, and generally less demand for tuk-tuks. It all added up to a more sensible day's work than his current situation. The TVs and karaoke that the foreigner had put in were all well and good for when he was on his break, but really, he was too old for the stuff the kids listened to, and it was an annoying distraction when he was trying to drive. He would much prefer a more basic and less technological tuk-tuk. His sister was a good woman and had never nagged him, unlike his wife who had very unreasonable expectations of him in terms of financial security. As a result, recently he'd even started sleeping in the tuk-tuk on days when he did have some money and was a bit less inebriated, just to avoid the old witch.

Oudom started up his Tuk-e-oke, pulled out from under his shady tree, and slowly trundled towards a petrol station. Having filled up the tank, he then slowly trundled his way to the outskirts of town where he found a good place to pull in and sleep for the night. The next day he headed north for his sister's. To facilitate the slight deviation from the routine his employers expected of him he had the good sense to take down the advert on the back for The Karot Rooftop Bar. As it occurred to no-one to look for him in a different province, including his wife, Oudom was never heard from again. Unfortunately, for Vince, neither was the Tuk-e-oke.

Tuk-e-oke number four.

Tuk-e-oke driver number four was a young lad called Leng. He had been recruited by Sophea at a time when Vince had been out, probably engrossed in a DVD store or something. Sophea had also devised a more specific job description for Leng, so that he was more of a night driver for the bar, rather than a regular out and about tuk-tuk-er. He was to remain on standby at The Karot should customers need to be driven home or get taken on to the next event of their evening's schedule. It meant he was also available for bookings with the Lucky Lucky Goose-Dragon Lucky Guesthouse, should they need to conveniently ferry their guests to the airport or the bus station. Vince was, at first, impressed by this innovation and felt Sophea was developing some very insightful business sense. However, it didn't take long to work out that Sophea was rather smitten with young Leng, and Leng was a little bit smitten with her as well. Instead of having a clear tuk-tuk based focus, he generally spent much of his time sitting at the bar trying to show off or clown around, with Sophea leaning on the other side and giggling annoyingly.

Vince had always respected Sophea and never thought that she would turn out to be a giggler. He had given her more credit than that, and she was starting to let him down. However, he was also prepared to concede that this was also an accepted social convention in the courting arena. In much the same way that young women in the UK were obliged to cheer from the cold side-lines of amateur Sunday league football games, whilst wishing they were warm inside watching the soap opera omnibus, it seemed that Sophea was culturally obliged to giggle like a high-pitched five year old at Leng's simple-minded antics. A side benefit to this courting ritual was that Leng seemed fairly happy to help fetch crates of beer up to the roof garden on Sophea's command and put the bottles in the fridge. Also, Leng's Tuk-e-oke had remained very much intact since he had taken on the responsibility, which currently was the exception rather than the rule. A final benefit was that Sophea, when not engaged in episodic giggling, had developed quite a happy and positive air about her, which was certainly more inspirational for the customers than her usual dower approach to human interaction. All in all, Vince was happy enough with the situation to go along with it all.

Tuk-e-oke driver number five, was Vince.

Tuk-e-oke number five.

Having learned a little about the tricks of the tuk-tuk trade, Vince had pulled up at the side of the street for an extended lunchtime siesta. However, unlike the lessons from the Mr. Oudom masterclass of inactivity, he'd worked out that the best place to achieve an uninterrupted snooze in the back of his tuk-tuk was by parking up at a busy market place. His tuk-tuk was one of many vying for limited customers, all of whom were actively chasing people from the market entrance and directing them to their own tuk-tuks. The chances of anyone actually trying to hire him in such a competitive and overwhelmingly enthusiastic environment was zero. It was the calm in the eye of the perfect storm.

Vince stretched himself comfortably across the back seat. He gazed out into the middle distance and contemplated his current trade-up. He decided that Tuk-e-oke driving should be considered an extra duty of being a Tuk-e-oke business owner. He was mainly doing it in the absence of a fifth candidate for the job, but largely he was reaching this conclusion because of his increasing awareness that letting an unknown quantity loose in one of his tuk-tuks was a far higher risk than he'd ever imagined.

As Vince had long since established, the trade-up was not just about employment, it was about the whole package. The job, the girl, the wheels, the pad, the threads – everything. The girl thing wasn't really on track with this particular trade-up. Maly was nice but they had philosophies that were way too different. No matter how cute Vince thought she was, she was never going to be cute enough to convert him to a spiritual plain where he was required to change his name to Jonah. Vince had very much turned a corner on that one, and his days of pursuing Ms. Maly were now well behind him. Wheels-wise, Vince, at this moment, was relaxing in his very own Tuk-e-oke. Not the most glamorous of rides, admittedly, and certainly not the most impressive form of transport from Vince's varied trade-up career. However, it was the first form of transport he had actually owned himself since selling his BMX to Luke Farrier for fifteen quid so that he could buy fireworks and let them off at the end of the street to impress his mates on Guy Fawkes

Night. How vitally important that had seemed then, and how irrelevant now. His pad at the top floor of the guesthouse was more than adequate for his needs. He still shared the top floor with his nan, but this was only fair. After all, she had shared her house with him for most of his life.

Threads-wise, Vince's current uniform was a grubby yellow baseball cap. This was traditionally worn in the street to distinguish the hireable two wheelers from the privately owned ones, and so it was easier for those who had to flag them down. His yellow cap then had to be swapped for helmet when going under-hire so that the squadron of police lurking on various corners had less reason to give him a hard time. Fortunately, 'Vince the tuk-tuk driver' had been an unlikely and disarming addition to the Khoyleng streets. The police stopped him a few times at first, largely as they had a sense that a foreigner driving a tuk-tuk was just all wrong, and so therefore probably they should. Having found that they couldn't get anything on him, as Mr. Vanarith had done all the paperwork, after a few weeks the police got used to Vince working his patch and generally left him alone.

The key difference with the current trade-up was that the business was his own. He was the boss and there was no other boss looking over him. In all the jobs that had preceded this one he had been working for someone else. In this one, sink or swim, it would be his decisions and innovations that determined the outcome. In a way. External factors, like the unreliability of recruited drivers, were also key in determining outcomes. However, as he was the boss, then he had the power to analyse and adapt his business plan to address these minor obstacles. There was an even broader and more satisfying implication to all of this. He was no longer living life as a bit part performer in the movie of someone else's life. A pawn in their story. Before, he had been Fairchild's gopher, helping Fairchild to live out his own playboy approach to business. Before that, he had worked in a hotel, a factory, a pub, and as a cabbie, all with the role of being a card in another person's deck. A couple of tuk-tuks and a small bar positioned over a badly named guesthouse might not be much, but it was all his. His life, and his ambition.

As Vince pondered nostalgically over the various elements of his spiralling success, he noticed that a young female tourist, who had been trying negotiate a ride in the tuk-tuk that was parked alongside his, was being mugged.

Danielle's year out

Danielle Fenton had been forced by her mother to take a 'year out'.

"A year out? From what?" she had asked. "Studying?"

Surely that was already a year out from making a meaningful contribution to society, or more like three years out. That was the impression that most of her fellow students gave as they drank, smoked, and lazed in bed watching day-time TV, and then pleaded with the lecturers to give them an extension on their essay deadlines. Danielle was genuinely concerned that there must be people out there more deserving of a year of aimless wandering around the exotic than herself. Overworked medical staff, traumatised policemen, underpaid factory workers, stressed counsellors, stressed people who received counselling.

The determination of Mrs. Fenton on this issue was absolute. Jacqueline Lehman's daughter, Imelda, had taken a year out and returned to the fold a much more interesting specimen than when she had been despatched. Danielle, meanwhile, was still a shy, uncomfortable kid whose main achievement was studying hard enough to get through university, and that was scarcely going to generate sufficient conversation to justify a permanent place setting at one of Mrs. Fenton's famous coffee mornings, particularly if the Lehman's were invited.

Mrs. Westwood's daughter, Gail, had been arrested twice for shop-lifting and once for joy-riding. At least that was interesting. Of course, Gail was never invited round for fear she might introduce some dirt to a spotless area of Mrs. Fenton's home or make off with some of the ornaments, but she was at least providing poor Mrs. Westwood with some juicy conversation. Danielle, meanwhile, when encouraged to contribute to proceedings, had once brought up the philosophies of Spinoza as a conversational starter with Mrs. Decker, who lived in Number 33 and worked in an accounting department. Mrs. Fenton had never been so ashamed and it had taken her the rest of the week to regain composure. No, that girl was going to get some real life experiences, and subsequently some engaging social skills, that were fitting for normal society. This wasn't just about coffee mornings. She needed to learn to communicate with the world in a polite and meaningful way if she was ever going to get anywhere. All this hiding away in her books just wasn't going to move her in to the social positioning that she needed at all. Imelda Lehman had evolved into a desirable young socialite and had enticed various handsome boyfriends that Mrs. Lehman perpetually cooed about. Danielle, meanwhile, had failed to bring anything home, handsome or otherwise, to be judged as to whether or not it was coo-able.

Subsequently, Danielle had been shipped off on her year-out to a range of expanding horizons and far off destinations by a tearful mother, who presumably had decided that an emotional send off would add some drama to the description of the departure at her next social gathering.

Danielle had started in New Zealand, having insisted that if she must go to a far flung corner, then her first travels needed at least to be in a country where she could understand some of what was being said. She had then bungee jumped off a high bridge, as it was on her mother's dinner conversation bucket list, and was so traumatised she had not been near either a bridge or a height since.

Danielle had then spent time in the Australian outback on a farm, trying to gather fruit that numerous oversized spiders and dodgy looking snakes had already staked a claim on, and were determined to defend at all costs. A number of her eight-legged adversaries then seemed to take it in turns to congregate in the back-packers' dormitories at night to prevent her from sleeping, as a strategy to further reduce her efficiency in stealing their fruit.

After Australia, she had experienced the Malaysian jungles and caught malaria. She had then experienced the Indonesian jungles and caught malaria. She had since been attacked by a monkey, had dropped her camera over a waterfall, smashed her watch whilst white water rafting and left her reading glasses on the plane to Feiquon.

In contrast, Imelda Lehman on her year out had seen the sun rise over Mount Fuji, which had been just the most wonderful sight she had ever seen. She had safari-ed in Kenya, where hippos had wandered through their camp at night, and when she looked out of her tent a baby hippo had been right next to her, which was just the cutest thing anyone could ever imagine. She had seen baby lion cubs, which apparently almost nobody ever gets to see, and she was *soo* privileged. Their guide had said they were just the luckiest group he had taken around the game park all year. She had witnessed a charming tribal people in South America, who had apparently mistakenly thought she was one of the British royal family after she told them that she was from England, as they had heard about the Queen, who came from England. It was just delightful and they had *soo* much fun. This was the tip of the iceberg of delightful, wonderful, cute, privileged, charming, and *soo* fun anecdotes that spewed forth from all corners of Imelda Lehman whilst guzzling coffee and grazing from Mrs. Fenton's selection of posh biscuits.

As her own journey progressed, Danielle gradually reached the conclusion that she must have taken her year out in a completely different dimension of time and space altogether, designed to balance out the perfection of the one that Imelda had enjoyed so much.

It was then no real surprise to Danielle at all to find herself being viciously mugged outside one of Khoyleng's larger markets. It was almost expected, in fact. She'd been in the city for a whole day without experiencing any violent wildlife, the loss of essential possessions (other than her reading glasses on the plane), or being infected by a life-threatening disease. It was, however, yet another reason to further resent her mother and despise Imelda Lehman, and yet another episode to add to the accumulating catalogue which would be an unfitting topic for either the dinner table or a tedious coffee morning.

Bag snatching

Vince was rather startled by his own athletic level of 'leaping to action'. He had always liked to think that in such a situation he would react at a useful speed and direction in an effort to aid a would-be victim of a crime. This was assuming that the crime was of a suitably low level of complexity and violence, and that meaningful contribution was possible without there being a pre-requisite for specialised training. However, until presented with such a situation, you never knew what your capacity would be.

Danielle had let out an incomprehensible yell as a young lad had tried to pull her shoulder bag from her. This had alerted Vince to the event and drawn him from his daydream. Danielle, who in recent times had become very wary of all situations, had been more securely attached to the bag than the assailant had realised, as it was hooked under her large backpack. Both she and the kid had fallen into the street as he violently grabbed it, assuming the bag would then be continuing in his direction on its own and without the owner still tied to it. Vince had arrived on the scene just as the attacker was starting to pick himself up and reach for the shoulder bag a second time, as it was now free from its entanglement with both its owner and her backpack. Vince ploughed into him with all the momentum that catapulting from the side of an adjacent tuk-tuk can provide. This additional unexpected collision meant that all three of them were then momentarily prostrate in the street, along with the contents of the shoulder bag, which were now distributed in an elaborate pattern next to the mugger. The young thief was still undeterred and swiftly rose to his feet for a second time. He swiped the exposed travel wallet from the road in one deft movement before leaping onto the back of his mate's getaway moto. Vince was also on his feet and giving chase. He wasn't far behind, and charged down the street as fast as he could, yelling what he believed in that moment to be the local equivalent of 'Stop! Thief!' although the odds of that actually being the case were incredibly unlikely.

By the time Vince returned to the scene of the crime, having failed to bring his pursuit to a successful conclusion, he found a tearful Danielle stuffing the remains of her distributed belongings into the remains of her shoulder bag.

Vince took a moment to bend forward with his straightened arms resting on his knees, acting as a couple of struts to prop his torso up while he tried desperately to regain his breath. A combination of a hot, humid climate, having his own bar, and having his own tuk-tuk service meant that there was no incentive to ever walk anywhere, let alone participate in exercise. As a result, his level of fitness was inappropriate for the intense workout he'd just exposed himself to. The impact of this aspect of his current lifestyle was increasingly apparent as he gulped down lungfuls of air in an attempt to recover to the point where he could try to be helpful. Eventually, he joined the distressed woman at the curb and got on his knees to assist her in the accumulation of the final scattered belongs, before attempting to engage with more formal communication.

"Yaw alright?"

Danielle looked up at him with tear-soaked eyes and an intense expression of contempt, which she usually reserved for when she was thinking about her mother. Fortunately, Vince was not deterred. Expressions of contempt were not an uncommon reaction for him when starting a conversation with an unacquainted female, and he'd developed a certain immunity to it.

"I just couldn't catch up to him, they were too fast. Still, at least they didn't get much."

The last few words of Vince's sentence petered out has he returned to a second bout of gasps and deep breathing.

"Didn't get much!"

Danielle was also used to her contemptuous facial expressions being bypassed, as this was a skill her mother had acquired and mastered over time. In response, her ability to quickly react with follow-up dialogue to reinforce these devastating looks was another tool within Danielle's repertoire.

"They got my travel wallet. That means they got my tickets, my money, they got my credit card, and my passport."

Vince was about to defend his original up-beat assertion about limited losses from the event. He had mentally compared the physical appearance of both the victim and the assailant. His brief sighting of the youthful thug that he'd just chased down the street enabled him to analyse the differences between the kid and the English girl who was currently kneeling in the gutter before him. On the basis of their utterly dissimilar appearances it seemed unlikely that the kid would get away with using her documents for identify fraud. He had been a grubby, short, skinny lad in his early teens, whilst she was a girl with long dark hair in her twenties. She may well also be considerably taller than the kid, but it was difficult to tell whilst she remained in her current hunched position in the gutter. Before Vince ventured to point this out, he quickly considered if there were any counter positions to this assertion. An alternative argument could be that airport security was not what it used to be, and for a few dollars distributed to the right person, cogs could get oily and grease the workings of any fraudulent and hair-brained scheme involving her passport and tickets. Clearly, on reflection, there were arguments and counter-arguments regarding the implications of how much could be achieved through misuse of the documents in question. Vince realised he'd said nothing out loud for far too long whilst working this train of thought through to its conclusion. He quickly decided to avoid the travel wallet conversation altogether, and take the discussion in a completely different direction.

"Where are you staying anyway? I can take you back to your hotel if you like. Sort everything out from there."

"I'm not in a hotel, you halfwit!"

Danielle gestured at the backpack that her mother had forced her to live out of, assuming it was obvious that, as someone who was traversing the city with all her luggage strapped to her, she probably wasn't securely checked-in to lodgings yet. She took a deep breath before continuing.

"Having tried and failed to find a cheap pair of reading glasses at the market, I was on my way to a backpacker's hostel. But now I've got no money and no I.D. So right now, no, I'm not staying anywhere!"

With that, the girl released a frustrated yell similar but slightly less violent to the one she had made when she was being mugged in the first place. Vince was increasingly aware that he and the mug-ee, whilst sitting in the street deliberating over the accuracy of Vince's accommodation assessment, were becoming quite a spectacle. Entertainment for the traders in a market place was as much a needed commodity as were any of the goods that they were selling. During the earlier period of launching himself at and chasing the skinny teen mugger, it had been as if the entire market in that instant had become a ghost town for all of the rallied support that intervened. Now that he was part of a drama involving an emotional woman on the floor at the side of the road, it was as if the entire city had encircled them to view the show. Vince was nothing if not patient, and decided to have a second go at being helpful.

"I own a roof top bar above a guesthouse. It's called The Karot. This is my tuk-tuk. Let me take you there, and we can use my phone to call the credit card company, and then call the embassy about your passport. You can then start to sort out the other things once those main worries are a bit more under control."

Danielle looked long and hard at Vince before eventually agreeing. She, too, was not enjoying her starring role in the ad-hoc market-place theatre. Meanwhile, the guy sat in the gutter next to her seemed harmless enough, and he had tried to help her. Besides which, she'd already been mugged, which he already knew, having been part of the event. The odds that he would be so stupid as to try to mug her again were fairly low, even by her unlucky standards. The bottom line was that she did need help. She didn't like to accept help as she was proudly independent, but this was the fact of the matter. The crushing defeat by the world at large against her self-esteem would never have happened to Imelda Lehman. The general absence of wonderful, cute, charming, *soo* fun muggers pretty much guaranteed it.

"She can sleep on the spare bunk in my pissin' room, so long as she don't snore too loud. I'm round at Vanarith's most nights anyway, Vince."

Vince acknowledged his nan's kind and generous offer, promised he would relay the message to Danielle, and gave her back her mobile phone, which he had used to call the British Embassy. He then returned to the table at the rooftop bar where Danielle was finishing her long and tedious conversation with the credit card company.

"Everything alright?"

Danielle nodded with the positive and reassured look of someone who knew that her bank account wasn't currently being emptied by a grubby teenager. Vince decided to continue with his news.

"I've spoken with the embassy. They say you need to call them back to confirm what I told them about the passport."

Vince slid a piece of paper across the table with the embassy's number written on it.

"But they say it is okay, and they can get you a new passport after next week. You have to go to the embassy tomorrow to fill in some forms, and then they can give you some temporary paperwork to use for identity while you're waiting. I can take you there in the morning."

Danielle picked up the paper with the number and smiled at Vince. She was starting to regret how harshly she'd spoken to him when they were outside the market. She started to put the numbers into the phone.

"Also, I've spoken to Mr. Piseth, who owns the guesthouse below the bar. He's happy to let you use a room for a week as there aren't many bookings at the moment. I imagine you wouldn't say no to a hot shower."

Vince produced the key to the room from his pocket and put it on the table.

"They'll also pick up any laundry you've got. Me nan just offered for you to bunk in with her, but I think you're probably better off with your own room for now."

"Well, that is very sweet of her, Vince, but having my own room with an en-suite sounds like heaven right now."

Danielle smiled again at Vince. All her contempt for him had dissipated. In fact, right now he had all the wonder, charm and cuteness of a character that could feature favourably in a dinner party anecdote. Vince continued to talk to her as he picked up the backpack and led her back down the stairs to the floor where her room was.

"I'll lend you some money for a few days, until you get your new credit card. I hope you'll join us upstairs for food later this evening, with me and Nan at The Karot. If you wander up around seven you can return my phone, and then we can have a drink first. Nan's been talking about making a steak and kidney pie, but I should try to avoid that option, as she has been experimenting with some very strange looking meat from the market recently and there's no telling what might be in there. Don't worry, though, Sophea can put together something less adventurous if you're after some comfort food. In the meantime, if you need anything else let me know. I'll be up at the bar."

Vince put down the backpack in the corner of the room and turned to leave. As his did so Danielle reached out and touched his arm.

"Thanks Vince. I really mean it. I'm really looking forward to a drink with you, and dinner."

Vince walked back up the stairs with a smile on his face. Clearly the Tuk-e-oke, along with its many other advantages, was a bit of a chick-magnet as well.

Vince's epiphany, part two

Danielle appeared at the bar looking like a new woman. Gone was the grimy college backpacker that Vince had found crawling around in the gutter looking for her scattered possessions. Standing before him now was an elegant, beautiful woman in a black dress. Vince smiled as she walked over towards him. Choc and Lamb, with a couple of their biker mates, looked on from the other end of the bar with expressions of mild astonishment. However, it was difficult to pinpoint whether it was the sight of Danielle or a mouthful of steak and kidney pie that had caused the partial contortion to their faces. Lamb seemed to have been working on a rather chewy bit of pie filling for a while and Vince only hoped that there would be no medical repercussions. The Dutchman would not be an easy person to carry down five flights of stairs to a waiting ambulance.

"You look great, Danielle."

"Well, I figured this dress has been stuffed at the bottom of my backpack for three months unused. Now is as good a time as any."

Vince joined her at the customer's side of the bar, having poured a couple of draft beers, and they began to chat. At first it was general, polite conversation about where they came from and what sort of things they did. As the evening wore on, Danielle became more comfortable with Vince's company and started to describe the frustrations of her critical mother and her enforced backpacking. Vince listened attentively as she unburdened herself of her woeful travelling tales. When talking to Vince, Danielle felt like a huge weight was being lifted. She finally had someone who seemed to understand and sympathize about her home life pressures.

The roof top ambiance settled into a late evening calm as the city gradually reduced its energy. The distant hum of occasional car horns against a background rumble of the remaining traffic, disgruntled guard dogs disturbed momentarily from their slumbers, and the faint rhythmic thuds of music from late night bars on distant streets became the backdrop urban cicadas. The

Karot had gradually emptied of regulars, but Vince and Danielle carried on talking into the night, delighted with the connection that they had made. Most people just thought Danielle was a boring girly swat whose mother was wealthy enough to throw numerous dinner parties, and so she had nothing in life to complain about. Vince seemed to understand that regardless of the situation, people always had pressures, frustrations, and emotions, making them as vulnerable as anyone else. As the time had passed, Vince had decided that they were very alike in many ways, and so he told her so.

"We'm a bit the same, aren't we? You're travelling around trying to 'discover yourself', as they say. I'm out here trying to see how I can change myself, and start to make it up further up the ladder."

"I don't see how that's the same at all Vince. Besides, I'm out here trying to discover the part of myself that my crazy mother would have liked to have as a daughter, which is slightly different from a desire to actually discover myself. But you, Vince, you're out here running around juggling a couple of dodgy jobs trying to scrape together a living. How can you say that those two things are the same as each other?"

Vince felt as though he should probably be offended by this remark, his sensibilities focusing particularly on the words 'dodgy' and 'scrape'. However, bearing in mind Danielle was a bit traumatised by her recent adventures, then maybe she just hadn't understood him properly. He decided to let her in on the whole trading-up scheme that he'd both invented and employed to further himself. In fact, it was very much a 'trade-up-plus' scheme these days since his epiphany on the back of the moto with Pastor Matthew. His trading up was no longer about crawling to a higher rung on a self-serving ladder. It was about quality of life and living your own dreams, rather than being a servant to someone else's ambition. He decided to add this extra annex to the epiphany aspect of his explanation as well, just to make sure she understood it properly the second time.

"It's not just about the trade-up, Danielle. Look at where I've made it to. I've got my own bar, which Mr. Piseth lets me run on the roof top of his guesthouse. I've got my own transport business, which I'm starting up with the tuk-tuks. Of course there have been some challenges, but that's to be expected. I'm an entrepreneur, Danielle. My own boss."

Vince paused. He'd never said all this out loud to anyone before. Now, as the words tumbled from his mouth in the form of actual sounds, he found that he was far less convinced than when it had been just rattling around inside his head. His inner monologue had described it all to him with far more authority and surety. Out in the open like this, it sounded more like an excuse for failure, rather than an inspirational speech to motivate others to follow suit. Having vocalised the entire scheme to someone else, basically he'd just talked himself out of the whole idea. Yes, it was true that he was his own boss, but for this to be the case he was also a poverty-stricken tuk-tuk driver, pootling around in the hot and fume-filled streets of a foreign capital. His fleet of five tuk-tuks was now down to two, as the other three had been crashed into a fish tank, set ablaze in a damp crossroads, and stolen by a barely-awake pensioner. His rooftop wine-bar, meanwhile, was one for which he had no lease or legal claim, so in reality it could be perceived that he was really just putting his energy into setting up a future business for the landlord. If the bar became popular then, no doubt, Mr. Piseth would start expecting most of the profits, or even take back the whole thing for himself. Vince certainly had no job security, and the current business scheme wasn't exactly making his fortune. So yes, he was his own boss, but boss of what? Also, was this set up really his own personal life-long dream: being manager and driver of a couple of pimped up mopeds? It was really a spin-off of Fairchild's dream of a chain of Asian hotels, which had since been abandoned by him.

Danielle had also thought for a moment about Vince's sage explanation on the meaning of life. The 'out loud' version hadn't sounded quite as desperate to her as it had to Vince. She decided to add her own views to the discussion:

"I see what you mean about being your own boss. Having your own self-determined direction in life. Not being a means to help someone else along their own selfish journey. I could do with some of that myself. My current life is mainly determined by my pushy mother and lots of studying, because that's what they told me I should do when I was at school."

"To be honest Danielle, now that I've explained my theory to you, and I've heard it out loud from myself, I don't actually believe a word of it. It sounds like a right load of rubbish. Yes, getting to be in charge of my own chosen lifestyle is what I want, but that's not really what I'm doing. I'm really picking up the pieces of Fairchild's guesthouse scheme, which in reality means I'm a kitsched-up tuk-tuk driver. I've been fooling myself with this whole trade-up nonsense. You're the one that has it sorted. You're studying something proper at university, and then you'll get a real career at the end of it."

Danielle remained silent for a moment, watching Vince as he unhappily contemplated his philosophically-devastating breakthrough. For a while there, her day had been looking up. Obviously it had started badly with losing the reading glasses on the plane, and then careered downwards a bit more with the street mugging. Since then, though, she had been rescued from the clutches of a roadside highwayman, and whisked away by her hero to a rooftop paradise. And now it seemed that before the night was out, despite his generosity towards her, she'd managed to destroy the entire reason of his being. Perhaps her pushy mother was right and her social skills did need working on a bit.

"I'm so sorry, Vince. I didn't mean for you to feel bad. After all, you've still had an incredible experience out here. It's like the year out that I was supposed to take, but never managed. You've learned a lot about yourself, who you are, what you want to be, gained some world experience, and seen a culture from the perspective of working with real people, not just by being a tourist. You can go back home a wiser person and really make something of your life. You might think that people like me have it all figured out, but what you've managed out here, learning what you want from life and gaining some confidence, was the sort of thing I was supposed to be doing, and look at how I failed at that!"

Vince was a little taken aback on learning Danielle's perspective. For once, his own failings were actually seen as enviable achievements by someone else.

Both of them thought long and hard, staring as the light from behind the bar played in the amber bubbles of their half empty glasses of beer. It had been a long day and they were both tired. Vince eventually mustered up the intellect to reach for the light-bulb of knowledge that had been dancing feverishly in front of his subconscious.

"It's a bit like, I'm doing the thing what you've been needing to do, and you're doing the thing what I needed to do."

Danielle nodded with a look that showed she was impressed with Vince's insight. Other than grammatically, she couldn't have put it better herself. There was not much else to be said on the matter, so she leaned over and kissed him instead.

Danielle's epiphany

It wasn't just Vince who had a whole niche epiphany thing going on. Whilst Vince had been mumbling his way around his vague theories on self-determination, Danielle had arrived at a minor epiphany of her own. She explained it to Vince over brunch at The Karot Rooftop Bar the next morning. She began with the wild declaration that she had never met anyone before who had made so much sense to her. This seemed rather unlikely to Vince, but he was aware that a bad hangover can easily cloud a person's judgement. His head was still ringing a bit from the night before, so no doubt she might have a similar impairment, which could lead to such a delusion.

"The point is, Vince, that you're right. You are leading the 'year out' that I needed. Your travels are part of your life, whereas I am really just a tourist playing short-term at being part of the culture. I've decided that I'll do a deal with you. Let me spend the next few months here with you, working at The Karot. It will be my first trade-up to a new lifestyle. A new job, new place, new threads…new man. If it works out, then we can go back to the UK and I'll help you find a business course, and then you can start to get your working life on track to where you want it to be. If you're on board with this you're not allowed to trade-up the girl though. If you agree, then there are going to be some new, strict rules to the trade-up system."

Vince nodded. It was probably about time for a review of the trade-up rules anyway. The current ones didn't seem to be contributing very dynamically to the overall aim of things. Also, he was delighted to hear that someone else was impressed enough overall with the broader trade-up concept to give it a try themselves.

"It sounds fantastic, Danielle. When do you want to start? We've got to go to the embassy later to sort out your passport, and then Mr. Vanarith needs to go to the travel agent to help you follow up on the ticket. Then we need to find you some new reading glasses, of course. You probably want a bit of a rest as well, and a look around city. What about next Wednesday?"

"Next Wednesday sounds wonderful, Vince."

Chapter 5. Business

Donor

It was the former Mrs. Ratcliffe that answered the phone. Unusually for Vince, he had actually planned ahead for this unfortunate eventuality. He knew he had to take immediate command of the situation, catch her off guard and get instant access to Mr. Fairchild. It was a tried and tested system used by many a young lad going back to their best mate's house the day after a fateful incident, such as a football going through a greenhouse window, or a prized flowerpot getting smashed as collateral damage during a game of Ackee.

"Yam right there, Mrs. Fairchild? Er, is Mr. Fairchild in today?"

"Is that Vince? No he's not!"

Vince's plan had failed. Susan had seen through the remorseful best school mate scam, and her icy tones had immediately conveyed that Plan A was already dead and buried. Vince was on the brink of hanging up when Susan made a long-distance lunge for him.

"Don't you start ringing here, Vince. We've finally got rid of you. Don't start coming near this family again. I mean it, Vince. Keep well away or there will be consequences. You know I'm not joking with you."

Susan then hung up the phone, removing Vince's need to do so. It had not gone well at all. Normally, the average parent suffering from the mounting collateral damage of two disruptive children becoming mates, eventually, albeit begrudgingly, allows her offspring to come out and play, having first delivered a stern warning about future behaviour. Unfortunately, Susan had never been average.

Vince felt a bit deflated, and decided to put off telling Danielle about his failure to secure a silent business partner. As with previous business ventures, Vince's limited networking had meant that he didn't have a large portfolio of associates to court once a business plan was developed. In fact, as with the original benefactor situation, when he'd first headed abroad, Mr. Fairchild was one of one.

It was a frustrating situation. Danielle had been working on their new business plan for weeks now. It looked really good, in fact it was impressive. Firstly, she had compared information on the internet about where tourists were going, what sort of tourists they were, and where the current supply of hotels for such people was unable to keep up with the demand. As a result, the small coastal town of Lomkevit was identified as a prime location. Vince was impressed. He would have probably started by asking people at the bar where they'd seen a place for rent, rather than analyse the markets. From this solid starting point of research by Danielle, she had then done lots of maths. Again, Vince was overwhelmingly impressed. The study looked at tourists' average budgets, their expectations in terms of service, and then reviewed what sort of rooms they wanted, at what rate, and where they were most sought after. She then went into the details to see what the running costs would be and the potential profits. By the time the document was finished, to imagine why anyone wouldn't want to invest in such a sure thing was beyond Vince's comprehension.

Vince sipped at a glass of beer as he gazed out from The Karot's roof top through the hazy, muggy air to the distant 'burbs. He couldn't go back to Danielle without at least some kind of Plan B of how to get some funding for her amazing ideas. There was no way he could let her down at this stage, especially has she'd devoted so much faith to his trading-plus epiphany. As he held up his beer and stared through the glass into the panorama beyond, deliberating on the matter through the golden distortion of his chosen refreshment, the phone behind the bar began to ring.

"Yaw right? This is Vince, at the The Karot.

"Vince. It's Jonathan."

"Mr. Fairchild. I was just trying to call you."

"I know. I overheard Susan's rather rude tone just now. I'd like to apologise for that, if I may. Susan's been rather difficult of late."

This was a turn up for the books. Susan had always been able to do no wrong in the eyes of her ensnared source of remarkable wealth. Maybe this turn of events was a chance for Vince and Danielle after all.

"No problem, Mr. Fairchild. I was just trying to get hold of you to discuss a business plan myself and my new partner, Danielle, have drawn up. It's along the same lines as before – setting up a guesthouse – but this time we've done all the research, and plan to set it up on the coast. It'll be in a place called Lomkevit. It's just up the coast from the main tourist town. Our research shows that it's the next up and coming place, so now's the time to get in. We've done all of the business planning for it. And we've got all the experience and learning from setting up The Karot Rooftop Bar, here in Khoyleng. Danielle, my partner, says if you can give us your email address then she can send the details, and you can see if you want to become one of the financial backers."

In recent months Fairchild had indeed become increasingly aware that the image Susan presented to him was not the full picture of the woman. The security of the ring on her finger had clearly over-stretched her confidence, and the occasional crack in the façade of marital perfection had started to show. A few times Fairchild had overheard the gardener getting an unnecessarily abusive dressing down. He'd also overheard the postman get it in the ear, following a letter getting delivered to the wrong house, and the electric meter reader receiving a rather unnecessarily unpleasant explanation of why he could have picked a better time to come round to perform his job.

Fairchild was becoming increasingly miserable. He'd let this woman into his life thinking she was the answer to all his wants and needs. Now that they were married, she'd started acting like she was some kind of feudal hacienda owner casting derision on to the suffering peasants. This wasn't the dream that Fairchild had envisaged. She had also started meddling in his business dealings, trying to make decisions for him, focusing on cold profit and diminishing his benevolent efforts. Since he had overheard Vince getting pushed off the phone earlier that day, Fairchild realised that Vince also fell into a category of one who deserved his benevolence, but had been clinically ousted from his generous support by Susan for her vindictive reasons. It was time to make amends and redress the balance.

As a result, Fairchild said that he was delighted to be asked to become a financial backer to Vince and Danielle's hospitality business plan. Not only was his enthusiasm for branching out into Asia renewed, but it was a chance to make amends for dumping Vince after he'd encouraged him to go out there in the first place. He promised to text Vince an email address that he knew Susan didn't have access to, and said that he couldn't wait to learn more.

Coast

Once the money was secured, the next step for the business plan was to find a suitable building to rent in the desirable up and coming location of Lomkevit. Vince once again applied his tried and tested approach of asking the only relevant person he knew. In this case it was Frank Schneider, who owned 'Die Englisch Sprechen Schule'. Frank, after all, was based in the main coastal resort town of Dhokratt, and owned a hotel overlooking the coast, for which Schneider had determinedly applied his imagination and, at length eventually named it 'Das Hotel An Der Küste'. It was about twenty kilometres from Lomkevit, so who better to advise Vince about his investment?

As it turned out, a couple of Frank's mates were looking to transfer their lease on a guesthouse in Lomkevit. They were a Belgian couple who had been running the now vacant guesthouse for five years. They had since decided they needed to head back to Europe, having achieved a youthful brood of post-toddlers, and decided that they now needed to seek out the family and educational support that Lomkevit was unable to supply.

Vince and Danielle jumped on a bus and headed for the seaside to check it out. As did Mr. Vanarith and Vince's nan.

The journey to Lomkevit was about six hours, but this was not Vince's first long-distance bus ride, so he was actually now recognising most of the karaoke songs, if not yet at the point of joining in to try to counter some of the distorted base with his own melodic tones. Regrettably, the same could not be said for his nan, who had clearly been practicing a couple of duets with Mr. Vanarith for just such an occasion, and relinquishing the microphone to enable other passengers to sing out-of-tune wasn't really on the cards.

The guesthouse itself was perfect. Positioned on the hillside with the ocean less than half a kilometre away, it featured a sweeping driveway leading up to the open and airy front porch, where views of coco-palms swaying on distant beaches mixed with the salty air from the warm breeze. The ground floor had a spacious foyer and reception, with a small bar, and corridors leading to six downstairs rooms and the kitchen. Upstairs there were a further eight guest rooms. Beyond the foyer, double doors opened onto an area of low decking, which led into a large garden lawn, bordered with flowerbeds, shrubs and bushy exhibits from arboretums. The previous owners had clearly been proud of their garden. The rooms were a bit shabby, but nothing a lick of paint couldn't put right.

As Danielle moved through the property she was already pointing out to Vince what changes would be needed, suggesting colour-schemes and contemplating furnishings. This was great news for Vince, as he was hopeless at that sort of thing. His most recent venture of pimping up the tuk-tuk was testament to that. However, immediately beside the decking that led onto the back lawn was an area that had previously sported a fishpond. This had been a key selling point for Vince. He'd grown rather fond of the goldfish in the fish-tank at the Carrot and Jam Kettle back in the Midlands. He'd even named two of the more prominent occupants Conrad and Simon; such had been the bond that had formed as he sprinkled the dusty fish-food into the top of the water. One of his missions was definitely going to be the renovation of the pond and the installation of new and exotic occupants. A bit of re-branding and advertising and The Karot and Coconut Guesthouse would be up and running.

The Mother

After weeks of cleaning, painting, fixing, mowing, furnishing and planning, the grand opening for The Karot and Coconut Guesthouse was finally about to happen. It would be a simple affair of sun-downers accompanied by a seafood buffet. Danielle and Vince's nan had been at the local market early that morning buying up a large amount of fish, squid, octopus and shrimp. It was going to be a long day. By evening, a number of invited guests were expected, including those they knew from The Karot bar, neighbours in Lomkevit and friends from the English language school. Vince had even invited trainee Pastor Matthew in an effort to swell the crowds.

As Danielle and his nan were in charge of the catering, Vince had been tasked with hiring a car and driving up to the airport in Khoyleng to fetch Danielle's mother. He'd not been looking forward to it particularly, as from the way Danielle regularly described her, Patricia Fenton sounded like a bit of an old battle axe. Danielle rarely talked about her father, and Vince had wondered whether Mr. Fenton's departure from the family had resulted from or caused Mrs. Fenton's obsession to compete her children's achievements against those of her neighbours, during which Danielle always came up short. Vince recognised that Danielle was a very clever and talented young woman, who had achieved a university place and was excelling at her studies. If this wasn't good enough for Mrs. Fenton then what on earth would she make of Vince?

Vince had made a cardboard sign saying 'Patricia Fenton' to hold up outside arrivals so that she could see he'd made an effort and they could start off on the right foot. He stood at the barrier, sign in hand and stared into the middle distance of the arrivals lounge, seeing if he could think of anything to talk to her about, at least at the beginning of the journey home. As he did so he heard a man's voice calling his name from somewhere to his side.

"Vincent, my boy. Is that you?"

Vince turned with the wholly unexpected revelation that he was standing next to Jonathan Fairchild.

"Mr. Fairchild! What are you doing here?"

"Wanted to see how it was all going. Thought I'd surprise

you and arrive at the guesthouse in time for the big opening. Things are a bit rocky with Susan at the moment, and I've always been excited to get into this guesthouse business, as you know. She was with friends for the weekend, so I thought I'd pop over and see how things are progressing. Anyway, now you're here we can go together."

"Well that's great, Mr. Fairchild. I'm just here to pick up Danielle's mother from her flight so she can come to the opening as well. We're having drinks and a small seafood buffet in the garden. There should be room in the hire car. It'll be no problem to give you a lift down to Lomkevit as well."

"That would sure be great, Vincent."

As they spoke, Vince became aware of a second and slightly exacerbated presence to the right of him. He turned to face a rather frustrated middle aged woman looking alternately between him and his sign with the annoyance of one who thinks she's being ignored.

"Mrs. Fenton. I'm Vince. How was your flight?"

"Tiring. I was stuck between a bawling kid and an old man who kept breaking wind."

Mrs. Fenton had the expression of one whose interest in social interaction had been very much diminished by recent events.

"Hello, Madam. I am Jonathan Fairchild. It sure is nice to meet you."

Vince's benefactor held out a determined hand, which meant Mrs. Fenton had to unload various bags onto Vince so that she could free up one of her own hands to participate in the shake. Vince, embarrassed that he had not initiated the introduction, felt that he should explain further.

"Mr. Fairchild's helping to finance the guesthouse business, Mrs. Fenton. He's been very kind to us. He's only just got into Feiquon as well. We'll all travel down to Lomkevit together."

Mrs. Fenton smiled one of those screwed-up face, pursed-lipped kind of smiles so that everyone knew it was forced rather than genuine, and then handed her final heavy suitcase to Vince.

"Well, let's get going then. I'm keen to see Danielle and find out how her travels have been going."

Damn, Vince thought to himself. He'd placed a lot of hope in making a good first impression so they get off to a good start, and it hadn't gone well at all.

The car journey didn't help much either. Fairchild was one of those people who insisted on giving the full update of all their news without hesitation, from the moment you'd last physically seen each other until the present moment you were being told the news. As the period of absence from each other's company had been considerable, this took quite some time. The monologue wasn't completely disastrous for Vince, as it saved him from trying to think up things to say to his girlfriend's mother. However, once Fairchild had finished with the news, he moved on to the reminiscing. As Vince and Fairchild's previous interactions were littered with accidents, chaos, misadventures and Vince briefly dating Fairchild's daughter, Vince didn't feel the reminiscing was going to help with the bond Danielle had sent him to develop with the mother.

On arrival at the guesthouse, Vince introduced Fairchild to Danielle, and then took him outside for a beer, to give Danielle and her mother chance to catch up. Within twenty brief and slightly uncomfortable minutes, Danielle and her mother had completely caught up. Vince then spent some time consoling a distraught Danielle in their room. Apparently the disappointments of Danielle's early travels, combined with the double disappointment of abandoning her travels and hooking up with this Vince character and the American bore with the overgrown moustache, wasn't going to provide suitable material for coffee morning one-upmanship with Jacqueline Lehman. Mrs. Fenton remained austere and chose to retire to the garden and immerse herself in a book while she waited for her daughter to regain some common sense. Sadly, the chances of getting a few pages turned quietly were undermined by the concurrent arrival to The Karot and Coconut of trainee Pastor Matthew. He'd been travelling since the previous afternoon, as it was the only way the buses connected, and so had arrived very early for the guesthouse's grand opening.

Vince decided he didn't have time to entertain the pastor, as he had to get Danielle's self-confidence back on track and Danielle back in the kitchen to work on the buffet. There was no way he could leave his nan unsupervised with experimental seafood preparation. Subsequently, he took the opportunity to introduce the pastor to Fairchild, who was milling about in the garden looking bored.

"Pastor Matthew, I'd like you to meet Mr. Fairchild. He's the businessman who is putting up the money for the guesthouse."

Trainee Pastor Matthew couldn't believe his luck, himself being a former businessman who had since put aside wealth for spiritual enlightenment. Fairchild was a very similar case to himself pre-enlightenment, and so was just the sort of person he should be converting. Also, Fairchild had a fascinating covering of facial hair in the sub-nose region. The pastor himself had a mole to the left of his chin that had a single wiry hair growing from it, which he had now cultivated to a length of about four and a half centimetres. With all these similarities their meeting couldn't be purely by chance, so he decided to take the plunge into cementing their spiritual connection.

"Mr. Fairchild, nice to meet you. As you know, 'The rich rules over the poor, and the borrower is the slave of the lender'."

The pastor ended, as he always did on these occasions, with a smug look and a slight flourish from his left hand.

Mr. Fairchild was momentarily puzzled. He wasn't used to an introduction to a guest at a gathering like this starting off with quite so much intensity.

"I'm sorry?"

"It's from Proverbs, Mr. Fairchild. It means that the evil of money can enslave men. I myself was once very successful in business, like yourself. I had lots of money, as you do, but now I only want to serve the people."

"Ah, I see, Pastor. Well in that case, perhaps I should reply by saying that 'I want to die a slave to principles. Not to men'."

It was the pastor's turn to form an expression of puzzlement. He wasn't used to getting quoted back.

"Is that from the gospels?"

"Nope, that's one of Zapata's."

The pastor quickly searched his memory of the scriptures, but struggled to pinpoint the book of Zapata. He was pretty sure that Zapata wasn't part of the Galilee crowd. He decided it must be Old Testament.

Fairchild continued:

"Emiliano Zapata was a Mexican revolutionary who fought for the liberty of the peasants, particularly their land rights. He had a magnificent moustache, a bit like mine."

The pastor hesitated again in light of the explanation, as he wasn't quite sure what to do with it. Or indeed what the facial-haired foreigner was talking about. He'd clearly unleashed something he wasn't prepared for. A quote, backed up by a moustache comparison, was a powerful thing. It also undermined his surety of their connection regarding his own protruding mole-hair. There was no one, to his knowledge from the scriptures, with a similar feature that could be called on to counter this profound observation.

The lack of response prompted Fairchild to plunge a second time into the archives of Mexico:

"Ignorance and obscurantism have never produced anything other than flocks of slaves for tyranny."

Fairchild paused for affect.

The pastor looked slightly horrified.

"Deuteronomy?"

"...Zapata. Again."

A boyish grin was spreading across Fairchild's face. His sudden enjoyment of the afternoon was in a small part due to the game of Mexican revolutionary top-trumps, but mainly because he enjoyed talking about Zapata, and especially quoting him. The pastor was clearly a man who enjoyed an exchange of interesting quotes and would make for good company while they waited for the evening's main event.

"Come and sit down. I'll tell you all about the feudal system that led to debt slavery in the haciendas, and Zapata's fight for agrarian land reform. Patricia, may we join you on the adjacent bench."

The pastor took a deep breath. This particular conversion was going to be hard work. Why did these things always have to be like some kind of test?

Patricia Fenton purposefully closed her book and put it on the seat beside her. She pursed her lips for effect once again, but Fairchild and the pastor were too engrossed in the banter to notice.

Vince returned to the garden a little while later. Fairchild and the pastor were in full flow, trying to out-quote each other, and Mrs. Fenton was looking incredibly irritated. However, if Vince knew one thing, it was that there's nothing so useful to neutralise a disappointed motherly figure as introducing another disappointed motherly figure, so they could compare notes and console each other. In the absence of that, Vince decided that his nan would have to do, and ushered her in to sit in the back garden next to Mrs. Fenton and join the gathering.

"Patricia, I don't think you've met me nan yet?"

Mrs. Fenton looked up and found herself face to face with a grandmother that smelled strongly of stale cigarette smoke, mixed with a slight odour of damp sea-fish.

"Pissin' hell, Vince, she's got her hair done just like Mrs. Barry had after she got confused down at Sharon Wells' salon and told her she wanted a 'bob', when she meant to say 'bouffant'. It didn't suit the shape of Mrs. Barry's face either, and it took ages to grow out again."

Vince cringed. He knew the dry and soulless sound of a coffin's final nail splintering its way into the mahogany when he heard it. On the bright side, though, things couldn't get much worse.

Opening night

Vince momentarily left Danielle in the preparation of spring rolls with crab meat and beansprouts, and peered through the kitchen window towards the rear of the guesthouse. Out on the lawn, things seemed to be going a bit better. The sun was low in the sky, cicadas were humming melodiously in the distance, and a warm breeze calmly flowed across the long grasses at the rear of the garden so they swayed like a gentle ocean current.

Fairchild and the pastor were still trying to out-quote each other with citations from their chosen idols. Sophea was milling around, absently pouring some very full glasses of wine. Frank Schneider and Wendelin had arrived and were sitting at a small table across from Mrs. Fenton making small talk, Choc was chatting to Maly next to the buffet table. In fact, it was all going remarkably well so far, considering how the day had started. Vince returned to the kitchen table where Danielle instructed him to arrange some prawns on a bed of lettuce, ready to join the selection of hor d'oeuvres to be passed around the invited guests.

Vince's nan was also in the garden, offering grilled octopus legs to trainee Pastor Matthew and Jonathan Fairchild. She had noted that Fairchild seemed to be avoiding anything that looked in any way slimy or tentacle like, and so she determinedly continued to push them on him, seeing it as part of the challenge. This was not because she felt he would benefit from the experience, but more because she was a bit bored and was looking for something to entertain her. Fortunately for Fairchild, her mobile phone started to ring and she stepped to the side to take the call, freeing him from having to politely decline the sucker-covered gooey mollusc-like extremities for the seventh time.

The call was from Mr. Vanarith. His absence was in part the cause of Vince's nan's boredom, as he had promised to get down to Lomkevit earlier that afternoon, but had since failed to arrive. As she listened, panic spread across her face. Brief but poignant information had been transferred to her often befuddled mind, and the news that she had received was not particularly good. She headed straight for the guesthouse, careering with a pelt that was a full as a woman of her years could muster, and burst into the kitchen where Vince and Danielle were putting the finishing touches on the display of king prawns.

"They'm comin' Vince! The pigs. They'm comin'!"

"What?!"

It was the shock of the surprise entrance, rather than the unlikely information, that had caused Vince to squeeze the middle of his current display prawn a bit too hard. The innards had shot into the back of a saucepan that was hanging on the side of the wall. In other circumstances the resulting 'ping' would have been widely classified as 'immensely satisfying', but sadly in this case it went largely unnoticed.

"The pigs! The'm comin'! Vince! Mr. Vanarith jus' called me, he's on his way down now. He says they were sniffin' round at Choc's place back in town. They know he's dealing. They pissin'-well know, Vince. They'm on their way here thinkin' he's coming down to make some big drugs delivery. Vince, they might pissin' think that we'm dealing as well!"

Vince thought about this briefly.

"But, you *are* dealing, Nan."

Vince's quizzical tone was not so much in relation to his own confusion, but more in trying to pinpoint whether his nan was genuinely aware that she was actually a minor and yet very real part of Choc's illegal distribution chain.

"What the *piss* are we going to do, Vince?"

"Well, we've got to tell Choc to get out of here, for a start, Nan. I'll go and find him."

Vince rushed out of the kitchen with the sole purpose of tracking down his trail bike mentor and providing the tip-off he needed to get out of Dodge. Instead he came face to face with Lamb, who'd recently arrived, and Vince nearly knocked his delicately gripped Cinzano and lemonade out of his hand.

"Lamb, you've gotta find Choc. Right now. The police have been searching round at your place back in Khoyleng and now they're on their way down here."

Lamb look dubiously at Vince. Further persuasive evidence was clearly necessary to sway the rigidly uninspired Dutchman.

"Mr. Vanarith is on his way. Now. He just phoned Nan. Says it's a drugs bust. Apparently he saw them going into your apartment."

Lamb, who initially appeared uncertain by the sudden and random information disseminated by Vince, seemed to accept the additional evidence and his scepticism swayed in the direction of hesitant belief. As he considered the potential revelation, he decided to provide Vince with some search options for the missing biker.

"Maybe he's gone to toilet. Maybe he's in the garden?"

It was enough for Vince to be getting on with.

"You check outside then, Lamb. I'll check the bogs."

Vince rushed off in one direction whilst Lamb strutted purposefully through to the back veranda and out into the garden. He stood on the low wooden decking and perused. As he did so, he was almost equally as shocked as he had just been about the apparent vulnerability of his Cinzano and lemonade. This burst of astonishment had occurred on spotting that, mingling amongst the throng of the garden party, was the love of his life. His grip on the Cinzano and lemonade became ever more tentative. She was wearing a blue silk gown that hugged her curves and covered up her ankles in all the right places. The distraction of this unexpected vision was all too much, and Lamb uncharacteristically let his emotions flow as he called loudly to her across the polite hum of bland socialite conversation.

"Wendelin! It is me, Babe. Your Lambikins!"

Wendelin, in a knee-jerk reaction, stood bolt upright, pouring an over-filled glass of chilled white wine into the lap of her husband as she did so.

"Lambert?!"

"The Dutchman!"

Frank Schneider, quick on the draw, had immediately put two and two together, added in some earlier suspicions, and the deduction, combined with the sensation of chilled chardonnay in his nethers, had resulted in him exclaiming a foreign national.

"Who are you?" quizzed Lamb.

"I am da husband. Schwien."

"Wendelin?!"

Wendelin leapt forward dramatically in response to Lamb's confused exclamation, and pointed an accusative chubby finger at Maly.

"Do not you start with this, Franklin. Ve know all very vell about you vith this vorthless self-righteous floozy of a voman!"

Maly stood up to protest. She was not accustomed to being called 'vorthless', or even a 'floozy of a voman'. Pastor Matthew stood up to stop her, but Maly pushed him violently out of the way. No amount of quoting obscure prose was going to interfere with Maly's gritty intent on a final showdown with her flaky-calved nemesis. It was bad enough the scabby-ankled bully had exiled her to the capital. But this wasn't work-time any more, and they were both on neutral ground. There was no way that this leech to her wonderful boss was going to lay into her in public without some resistance, and especially with Frank there to hear it.

Lamb wasn't good at arguments, but he'd been in enough to clearly foresee where this one was heading. Regardless of the immediate progress of the current heated debate, Lamb knew that it was always best to make sure you threw the first punch. If it was a good one, it would reduce the number that would later be aimed at you.

Before Frank could overcome the hesitation of whether to defend Maly or get angry with Lamb, he took the full force of a swipe from the Dutchman squarely in the cheek and found himself careering horizontally in the direction of the trainee pastor. Having forcefully connected, the pastor then careered into Sophea, who duly covered him in a tray full of papaya salad and chilli sauce before he eventually collided with the oeuvre-laden buffet table.

Fairchild stepped in to try to calm the situation. Choc stepped in to try to make it worse. As he did so, Lamb remembered why he'd rushed into the garden in the first place.

"Choc, we've got to go. Vanarith called. Says policemen are on the way to arrest us. Says that they already searched the flat."

Choc didn't need telling twice. Even if there was quite a fruity punch-up developing in which he quite fancied a tumble. Both Choc and Lamb rapidly assessed the situation. As it stood, Frank was getting to his feet looking dizzy. Pastor Matthew was prostrate on the shrimp vol-au-vents. Maly had now got Wendelin in a headlock and was trying to pull out clumps of her pasty red hair. Fairchild was flapping around like a disfigured ostrich and Sophea was trying to recover what remained of the soufflé. The current balance in the ensuing struggle wouldn't last long, and clearly the Germans would soon regroup, although whether this would be with or against each other was difficult to judge.

A quick exit was definitely in order. Choc quickly trotted across the lawn and up the few steps to the veranda decking, followed by Lamb. He reached for the door at precisely the moment that it violently swung open with the force of at least three hurricanes. His hand, followed by his arm, smashed through the cheap glass of the door and continued forward through the jagged shards, up to the point that his head collided with the wooden frame. Despite this opposition to its movement, the door still retained sufficient thrust to transfer the necessary momentum to send Choc staggering backwards, where he tripped over the edge of the decking and landed in the shallow fishpond below. As if the dramatic splash had been the gong to announce the arrival of an important gladiator at a Roman arena of carnage, a formidable figure stepped forward through the broken doorway and pointed accusingly at one of the guests.

"Fairchild!"

The uninvited guest

"Susan! But how?!"

Susan Ratcliffe bristled with a stiffness and anger that most Roman gladiators, or bristles, would have been hard pressed to compete with. The door fell off its hinges behind her, causing more of the glass to smash, as if in recognition that it had come up against a foe for which capitulation was the only option available.

Vince had just arrived around the side of the guesthouse, followed by Danielle, still in their desperate bid to locate Choc before the police did. The presence of Susan bristling formidably across the veranda overshadowed both the fact that they'd finally found Choc, and the fact that Choc was prostrate and semi-conscious in Vince's new fishpond. Vince had never seen anyone bristle before. It's a phrase occasionally bandied about, but often by those with limited experience of the phenomenon. Until someone's bristled to the degree that Susan currently bristled, and done so directly in front of you, then you can't possibly appreciate the subtle undercurrents and fearsome nature of the whole thing.

"If you think I can't track your every move by getting daily updates from the credit card company and the bank, then your underestimation of my skills and talents as a wife is even greater than I realised!"

Vince shuddered.

Choc also shuddered, but this was more due to the coldness of the pond and the unfortunate position of a particularly enthusiastic barbed catfish.

Susan began to stomp menacingly in the direction of Fairchild, who had just been considering starting a brawl with Pastor Matthew, as a less violent alternative to what was about to come.

Meanwhile, Frank was back his on feet and heading purposely for the veranda to catch up with Lamb.

Frank's judgement had been poor, and he did that thing when two people are walking towards each other and get all hesitant as they both try to get out of the way by moving to the same side. Unfortunately, Susan was in no mood for compromises, and with her predatory instincts in full flow she was more than psyched up with the adrenalin that was needed for a newcomer to claim their corner in an established punch-up. Consequently, Frank found himself in horizontal flight for the second time in as many minutes. Once again, he connected with the pastor, and this time the force was sufficient to provide both of them with the momentum to maintain a trajectory that took them deep within the branches of a large ground-hugging pine tree, where they completely disappeared from view.

Vince and Danielle rushed to help Frank and the pastor, leaving Lamb to assist the damp and bruised Choc to address his catfish imposition. Vince pulled Frank out from the depths of the needled branches, whilst Danielle helped the trainee pastor his feet. They emerged from the foliage with the immediate intention of assessing the situation. However, the opportunity was lost as Vince's nan arrived at dramatic speed on the veranda with a declaration of her own.

"The pigs! The'm pissin' 'ere!"

The garden party stopped in suspended animation and stared at Vince's nan. Vince's nan momentarily stared back at the scene of developing carnage. When she had left, only moments before, it had been a polite gathering of gentle conversation and elegant social patter, with an element of enforced experimental seafood tasting. She could therefore be forgiven for the double-take as she tried to work out if she'd taken a wrong turn and made her dramatic announcement at a neighbouring garden party. What immediately caught her eye was Wendelin, who had turned the tables on Maly's wrestling advantage. She was on the grass, prostrate on top of Maly, had her in a head lock, and was now leading the hair-pulling, rather than being subjected to it. Vince's nan had become fond of Maly over recent months, largely due to Maly's apparent interest in the modern history of UK-based TV game shows. Instinctively, she abandoned all memory of her shock announcement, and launched herself from the decking. In the same way that a ring-tailed lima might disembark from a perfectly sturdy trunk onto a springy branch and then catapult again in a wistful manner at a distant but broadly girthed and insect blighted tree trunk, Vince's nan joined the skirmish. The final destination in this particular foliage analogy was Wendelin.

Unlike his nan, Vince chose to focus on the police element of the latest update, and rushed forward to re-assist Choc, releasing, as he did so, his current grip on the slightly swooning Frank Schneider. Frank staggered backwards and disappeared once again into the dark depths of the peripheral undergrowth.

Lamb was already pulling Choc from his watery collapse and dragging him out by his remaining good arm. When Vince reached him, he helped by giving Choc a final shove from behind, and then assisted in removing the catfish.

Danielle, gobsmacked at the whole event, let go of the disorientated Pastor Matthew, who also staggered backwards and disappeared back inside the all-enveloping pine tree, reasserting his residential status beneath the sweetly odorous branches next to the incapacitated Frank Schneider.

Maly, who was now free of Wendelin, as Vince's nan had taken up the cause and joined the tag team, observed through her fuggy vision that Danielle had apparently deposited the pastor and spiritual leader of her questionable church into some nearby foliage. In her heightened state of violence, she came gunning with all she had for Danielle. To her surprise, her impending attack was immediately cut off in its prime by Sophea, who had been standing on the fringe of current events in her capacity as drinks and hor d'oeuvres distributor. Sophea wasn't one for violence, or significant action in any form the vast majority of the time. However, Danielle was the co-boss of the current half-baked guesthouse scheme that she'd unwittingly followed Vince on, so Sophea's immediate livelihood was considerably linked to the girl's survival. Due to recent events, Sophea was brandishing a large, but now empty, aluminium tray in her hand that, until a few moments before, had displayed a rather spicy papaya salad. Maly was already fairly out of it, so a good strong swipe from Sophea with the metal tray connecting squarely in the face was all it took to bring her down.

Danielle's mother had also been on the periphery of the developing antagonisms, desperately trying to work out who was who in all of this, so that she could pick a side. The arrival of Sophea to defend her daughter helped her with the decision. Danielle's safety would come first, of course. However, as her daughter was clearly well defended already, the ally who needed the most support in all of this was Danielle's benefactor, Fairchild, who was cowering like a scolded puppy before some permed and ranting peroxide nightmare from the '80s. Mrs. Fenton marched up to Susan and pushed her hard on the shoulders, so that she fell backwards on to the ground with a thud. Anyone currently not involved in a full-on fracas – of which numbers were limited – shuddered as they reassessed the value they assigned to their own coccyx. Susan looked up in disbelief as Mrs. Fenton took the stage to launch into a rant of her own.

"Who on earth do you think you are, Blondie?! This kind man has helped my daughter and Vince to start up their business, and you have the nerve to come into this soiree, talking to him like that, and treating him like dirt. I'm disgusted to think that you and I originate from the same country. You'd never get an invite to one of my coffee mornings! Common as a garden toad!"

Susan continued to gaze up at Mrs. Fenton, absolutely stunned. The wind was completely knocked out of her sails.

Fairchild beamed at Mrs. Fenton in total awe. Now this was a real woman!

It was just as Susan was rapidly reassessing her strategy and planning her next move that a considerable number of policemen reached the rear of the building. Having quickly gained an overview of the battlefield, the police, who were not particularly bound by the kind of constraints that prevent the constabulary in the UK from showing copious amounts of spontaneity and initiative, simply arrested everyone. Their thoroughness in identifying potential arrestees even extended to those amongst the gathering who were otherwise lost and unconscious, hidden beneath the dark and heavy lower branches of the pine tree.

Cell

The freshwater aquatic community of Asia largely rely on oral histories to maintain the continuity of their cultural identity, and subsequently have not developed a written script within the diversity of their linguistic traditions. Therefore, much as the catfish that had recently encountered Choc Cadby would have appreciated the chance to use the popular psychological technique of writing a letter to himself to articulate his mental trauma, work through the emotional scaring, and eventually cast away the missive so as to expunge himself of the whole event, he had neither the cultural evolution nor the academic skill sets to do so. Also, the paper would have got very wet. However, communication of emotion and trauma was not a constraint that might have disempowered a number of the visitors to the Dhokratt police station that evening.

Susan had perhaps been the most vocal in her disagreement with the authorities regarding her incarceration. The chief of police had sat quietly and tolerated about forty seconds of her abusive rant before making the decision that Susan Ratcliffe would be the first of his visitors to be locked in the single cell at the back of his office. It was an unusual decision, considering the raid had been specifically to round up a couple of small-time smugglers. However, having experienced the woman, he felt fully justified in his decision.

Wendelin's protest at her arrest had been the one that captured the most physical expression of emotion, as she had lamped one of the unfortunate junior officers, as he was encouraging her beloved Lambert to join them for the short journey in the back of the pick-up to the constabulary's local headquarters. Consequently, despite the lack of facilities, the police had wisely placed the violent, but dermatologically-challenged German in her own isolated cell, which involved blocking her up in an old, but sufficiently spacious, chicken coop at the back of the yard, using a couple of bags of cement against the door to secure her in.

Fairchild had recovered a sense of dignity and importance once Susan had refocused her energies on the authorities, and was desperately trying to console Patricia Fenton. Danielle's mother had been struck with the sudden realisation that not only would her arrest impact greatly on her social circles in terms of coffee morning gossip, but would actually put her in the same category as Mrs. Westwood's shoplifting daughter Gail, who was specifically taboo from all socially-charged caffeine-related pre-noon gatherings.

For Vince, it was particularly handy that Mr. Vanarith had not arrived at the guesthouse in time to be arrested. Considering that Mr. Vanarith's particular skill was organising documents and payments to help administrative cogs to function, or even bypass them all together in favour of a more lucrative cog, his delayed presence at the beach resort was particularly convenient. Vanarith did, however, make it to the police station about half an hour after the rest of the garden-partiers, and his first achievement was to financially convince the chief of police that as proprietors, Vince, his nan, Danielle, Patricia, Sophea and Fairchild were the victims in all of this kerfuffle. They were innocents trying to bring business to the community, to help with national investment and local employment. They should be applauded for their selfless contribution, rather than arrested for their accidental association with shady guests. They were the victims of the circumstance rather than the perpetrators. Following this explanation and a little bit more under the table national investment and local employment, the six victims from The Karot and Coconut Guesthouse were released from custody with no charges brought against them.

Frank Schneider was released even before Vanarith had talked the police chief into letting the others go. The Chief of police had quickly realised that amongst the arrestees was his benefactor, who provided the *Das Hotel An Der Küste* function room free of charge for the annual police new year karaoke seafood extravaganza. However, the chief was less inclined to be sympathetic towards the muscle-bound yob and wife of the hotel owner, who had knocked out one of his junior staff. As a consequence, Frank reluctantly spent the remainder of the night spraying industrial-strength insect repellent through the darkness and tangle of chicken coop wire in response to the hum of nocturnal creatures as they indulged their curiosity in the combined scent of bird shit and Wendelin's ankle perspiration.

Pastor Matthew, along with Maly, were also released, shortly after the verbose cleric had regained sufficient consciousness to start delivering obscure quotes about religious persecution, for which the tired chief neither had the patience or the interest.

Who were of interest to the Dhokratt Chief of Police were the two foreign gentlemen known to him as Choc Cadby and Lambertus-Wilhelmus Timmis. The chief had been in regular communication with the police team that had raided the two bikers' Khoyleng residence, as well as the sergeant who had led the team in visiting Choc and Lamb's remote village retreat and warehouse in the forest. The remaining human collateral from the garden party raid that his officers had efficiently decided to net was more of a distraction from the real matter at hand. However, in his empathy for the people of the country that he served, the chief was inclined to hold Susan in the cells for an extra day before deporting her in a police van directly to the airport in Khoyleng, so that as few people as possible had to encounter her. He got the impression that the rich American guy that had difficulty shaving his upper face might even contribute to some of the funding for that.

Earlier that day, Mr. Vanarith had seen the police raids on Choc's place in Khoyleng. He recognised that the extent of their arrest was slightly too inter-departmental and high-profile for him to start getting actively involved. Any attempt to influence decisions or supply documentation could result in him suffering the repercussions. He did, however, phone up a couple of lawyers he knew back in the city, and asked them to come the next day to Dhokratt to give Choc and Lamb some legal assistance. After all, Mr. Vanarith had supported Choc to get his paperwork for setting up the trail bike business in the first place, and so a couple of well-placed legal types floating around wouldn't do him any harm either.

It was around 11.00pm when Vince and his extended family finally returned home in the back of a police van, having stopped at the petrol station in Dhokratt to give Vince the chance to fill up the fuel tanks as part of their fee for the return trip.

Vince slumped into a chair next to Danielle.

"I'm so sorry things worked out like this. We were trying to get away from the bad things that happened on your 'year-out' and now you've ended up arrested and nearly spending the night in a cell."

Danielle grinned back at Vince.

"What are you on about, Vince? That was fun. No wandering aimlessly about and suffering touristic disasters on my own. This is being part of it; not observing a culture, but living it. Seeing life as it really is!"

Vince was about to express scepticism at this response, but stopped himself, deciding it was better to avoid rocking a non-problematic boat. He tried to freeze his expression into one of mild contemplation instead.

Danielle leaned across to Vince and whispered in his ear.

"Also, my mother got arrested and I was there to see it. My life will never be quite the same again!"

Departure

Six months later...

Vince's business course registration was complete. He would start in two weeks' time. Danielle had been the careers adviser he'd never had. The only career advice he'd previously received was from his physics teacher telling him to go to sixth-form to study physics and be something to do with physics. He now realised that this was because the job security of his physics teacher relied heavily on him keeping the numbers up in his A-level classes, rather than any desire to seed Vince's successful advancement into a world of scientific endeavour.

To be fair, Vince had since realised that many of his teachers had no idea about careers in the real world either. He felt that most of them had probably drifted aimlessly through education, albeit more successfully than him, and gone to university studying a subject that was largely irrelevant to anyone outside of academia. In the absence of any decent career advice being imparted to them, they subsequently returned to their scholarly comfort zone to complete the unadvised career circle. One or two had, no doubt, genuinely aspired to teach and inspire their students in their chosen subjects. However, the tunnel vision for these individuals, in relation to their ability to impart broad knowledge regarding careers in the world at large, was perhaps even greater, as they'd not even been challenged to consider deviating from the education sector. Vince certainly hadn't come across any of this rare species of teacher whilst he was failing at being a sixth-former.

Things were different now. Danielle had helped him to find a bridging course, and once completed he would be taking a degree in business management at the same university as her. He would even get some financial support for it as well.

Meanwhile, Danielle had never been happier. Vince was her soul-mate. She may not have discovered how to cope with her mum's dinner parties, but she had discovered Vince. In fact Vince might well be a much needed additional element of despair for her mother's social gatherings, should their future presence ever be requested. Good. They could disappoint her mother as a team. Danielle had loved working at the bar, and then running the guesthouse, but most of all being with Vince. She was now far more confident in who she was, and where she was heading which had never been the case before. She was ready to take on the world, and that included her mother.

Vince's nan and Mr. Vanarith watched the plane from the viewing deck as it ambled down the tarmac. Having lined itself up at the start of the runway, the jet engines took one last big breath and, despite the mid-day heat, decided to go for it anyway. Gradually the aircraft left the ground and climbed up towards the clear-blue and its endless possibilities.

"These young kids today are far too pissin' serious, Vanny. It's all about success with that lad. Business this, profit that, pissin' the other. They want to learn to pissin' well enjoy themselves a bit more. Come on, Vanny, let's go back and run that guesthouse of his, and together we'll have some real fun!"

The Riviera

Jonathan Fairchild stood near the prow on the upper deck of the Emiliano. It was his favourite of the cruise-liners he had invested in for ferrying wealthy tourists around the Mexican Riviera, so that they could become connoisseurs of locally brewed Tequila and desperately hot chilli sauce. He leaned against the white-painted steel rail, inhaled the salt air, and gazed wistfully across the ocean. The setting sun spread its kaleidoscope of warm, broken colours across the rippling expanse between them as if reaching out in friendship. The sense of contentment and satisfaction that brewed in Fairchild's soul might have been how Emiliano Zapata had felt after a victory over the feudalist landlords. An overwhelming sense of achievement, combined with the satisfaction that you were exactly where you were meant to be, and most importantly, with the people you belonged with. Was it mere coincidence that he should find himself back on the Emiliano after his great adventures in Europe and Asia, and that, despite the twists and turns of his travels, he had returned triumphant? He was no longer a confused and lonely man of wealth, a man with everything, and yet nothing. Now he was a player, with a vigorous lifeblood coursing through his very being, a tenacious purpose and meaning to his life. As he stared at the disappearing sun, basking in his self-congratulatory reverie, a glamorous and perfectly styled figure in a beautiful blue evening gown appeared at the side of Jonathan Fairchild, and linked her arm in his.

"Come now, Jonathan, it's time we made our way over to the Zapata dining hall. We are expected as guests of honour at the captain's table. We can't keep him waiting now, can we darling? After all, he is throwing this wonderful dinner party for us."

As Fairchild turned to Patricia Fenton, she gently straightened his bow tie and delicately kissed his cheek. Jonathan smiled back at her. It gave him great pleasure to see his new-found love enjoying herself on the Riviera cruise so much. It was clearly the life she had always been born to lead. Patricia had a real talent as an organiser and as a socialite. She could effortlessly judge what to say, and when to say it. She knew how to make people feel welcome, who needed to be introduced, and what insights enabled people to chat to others and comfortably enjoy new company. Most importantly, she delighted in every detail of this social weaving. Fairchild was endlessly fascinated in Patricia's concern over who would sit next to whom to ensure all the guests had the most engaging conversations and most pleasant evenings. It was almost a shame she wasn't a regular member of the crew, so that the guests could benefit from her well-crafted dinner party organisation on the Emiliano every night.

Fairchild turned and gently pulled Patricia closer, before beginning to walk her back towards the restaurant area and the throng of guests as they prepared for dinner.

"I've been thinking about how much you seem to be enjoying the social life on board the ship, Patricia. Indeed, both you and your daughter have a real flare for hospitality and social management. Maybe this type of work could be a real opportunity for Danielle. Once she's finished at university, perhaps she and Vince could get into cruise ship management."

Patricia Fenton gazed up at Jonathan, her expression morphed into one that was both sceptical and yet at the same time quizzical and intrigued.

Patricia mentally weighed up the arguments. The delight at the one-upmanship that could be achieved in inviting Mrs. Lehman and her daughter Imelda to dine with the captain of the cruise ship that was managed by her daughter was almost overwhelming. On the other hand, of course, there was Vince.